The sunshine pierced Giles' eyelids and the twitter of little birds penetrated his skull as if a ring of woodpeckers was drilling holes into his brains.

Groaning, he threw back the covers and almost threw himself out of bed. He trudged down the stairway, feeling incredibly heavy and clumsy, and headed for his mirror at the landing to assess the damage. *Dark circles*, he figured. *Bags and wrinkles. I shall be shocked at how old I look.*

But what he actually saw was far more shocking.

The face that reflected back at him was not that of an aging man who hadn't had enough sleep. It wasn't even a man's face.

What it was, was monstrous: It was enormous and scaled, a leathery, grotesque conglomeration of inhuman features set in an elongated head rather like that of the Alien in those films by Ridley Scott. His oversized ears were tufted, and large, thick horns like those of a ram curled around the face.

With shaking hands, he explored his features, distressed to realize that the nightmarish creature in the glass was doing the same. It was he, and no mistake.
I'm a demon?

THE JOURNALS OF
RUPERT GILES

Vol. 1

Nancy Holder

POCKET
BOOKS

LONDON · SYDNEY · NEW YORK · TOKYO · SINGAPORE · TORONTO

First Pocket Books edition February 2002

™ and © 2002 Twentieth Century Fox Film Corporation.
All rights reserved.

POCKET BOOKS
An imprint of Simon & Schuster
Africa House
64-78 Kingsway
London WC2B 6AH

www.simonsays.co.uk

This is for the GASPERS and the fearless folk of SPAGHETTI (and you know who you are!)

Acknowledgments:

Ripper and Holder would like to cordially thank:
Mr. Anthony Stewart Head, Joss Whedon, Caroline
Kallas, and the entire staff, cast, and crew of BTVS;
Debbie Olshan at Fox; Lisa Clancy, Liz Shiflett,
and Micol Ostow of Simon & Schuster; literary
agent Howard Morhaim, and Florence Felix, his
assistant; and, especially, the authors of the scripts
novelized for this book. Thanks to Allie Costa and
Angela Rienstra and Pat-mom. And a huge thanks
to Michael Reaves, without whom. . . really.

PROLOGUE

Rupert Giles had finished drawing his magick circle in the woods outside the small California town of Sunnydale. Its Spanish settlers had originally called it Boca del Infierno—the mouth of hell—and that name had been more honest. Sunnydale sat on a hellmouth, a portal to the demon dimensions that bulged with evil beings that longed to reclaim dominion over the earth, which had been theirs first. Its miasma called to creatures of the night both near and far, fairly littering the cemeteries and shadows with their ilk—giving Buffy the Vampire Slayer no rest as she fought them, night after night after night.

And I?
I Watch.

Now he sat inside the perimeter of salt, his incantations complete, and turned to a fresh page of his journal. He took up pen, and hovered for a moment over the traitorous passages Dawn and Spike had read, thereby discovering the truth about Buffy's "little sister."

God help me for my negligence. She ought never to have found my journal, much less learned of her origins in such a terrible way. It was already practically impossible for Buffy and me to believe that she hadn't always been here.

No wonder she tried to annihilate herself.

However, it's not at all difficult to believe that the whole wretched affair occurred on Buffy's birthday. But how can it be that every single one of the reigning Slayer's birthdays—at least, since I've been her Watcher—winds up such a bloody mess? Is it simple bad luck, or are there forces at work I've not yet pinpointed?

Is it because she lives on a hellmouth?

Is it something about me?

More importantly, what can I do to stop them from becoming even worse? Because I simply don't know if she can survive another one. . . .

He stopped writing for a moment, reflecting on his task. Men and women such as Giles were required to write almost obsessively in their journals, in the hope that whatever knowledge they gleaned during their tenure as Watcher to the current Slayer could be passed on to the next slayer. That there would be a next slayer was a sad but accepted fact; slayers rarely survived past their mid-twenties.

He frowned and added:

She's only twenty, damn it. And my Buffy ought to live for years yet; decades, if I've anything to say about it.

In fact, that is why I am here, to summon Krathalal, even though I realize it's forbidden to do so, and that if it is discovered that I have done so, the Council will be in full possession of their rights to have me killed.

However, as Quentin Travers once put it so eloquently,

I have a father's love for Buffy, and that cancels out all else.

Signed on the night of the Slayer's twentieth birthday,

Rupert Giles, Watcher

He closed the journal and regarded it for a moment. Like he himself, the notebook was not prepossessing. One would never guess it contained arcane secrets of other dimensions, the Black Arts, and magicks forbidden to human eyes for centuries. *Ah, but you can't judge a book . . . or a man . . . by his cover.* A Watcher always lived a double life; first he had been the high school librarian, then rather cast adrift; now he was the Watcher again, reinstated on Buffy's own insistence as together they fought Glory the Hellgod. His whole life had been fashioned to accommodate the needs of his Slayer, even of his waiting to be Called to the esteemed position. He'd tried to fight that destiny, and ultimately surrendered to it.

And it cost me, dearly.

He thought of Jenny Calendar, dead in the earth these three years, and sighed heavily. He would always miss her. Always love her.

He drew on his black wool cloak and threw the hood over his head. It was the same clock he'd worn in his London days, after he went down from Oxford. Then with great care he opened the carved wooden box on his left and drew from the glittering black velvet nest a wickedly sharp curved knife. His gaze focused on the bronze hilt, which depicted the hideous demon Krathalal, Ravager of Souls.

The demon's angular face was mutilated with deep gashes that, according to legend, never stopped bleeding. His two eyes, yellow-glowing and reptilian, were split into halves and, in the center of each, a tiny minion crouched. When Krathalal caught a soul, he would suck the essence from it and fling the tattered remains to his eye-minions, who would use them to dab at the bloody wounds on the demon's face. These in turn were given to Krathalal's large family of wives, sons, and daughters. Each of these ruled over one malady or ailment that afflicted the living beings of the world, animal or human.

Krathalal also drank the blood of the living, much as a vampire would. When it was made to him as an offering, he would often do his supplicant's bidding . . . if the blood was rich and hot.

Tonight, Giles worried that his blood was water-thin and ice-frozen. He raised his left hand, palm facing himself, then slashed it. The pain made him wince, but he slashed it again, and then a third time, this one directly transecting the first two. The pain from the wounds caught him low in the belly, and as perspiration beaded his brow, he turned the hilt and pressed Krathalal's bronze face against the wound. The metal lips parted, and the mouth began to suck.

"Demon Lord Krathalal, I summon you," he proclaimed. "I demand of thee, dead lord, that you accept my sacrifice and deem me worthy of a boon."

The hideous knife kept drinking. Giles remained still, though the knife began to warm, then heat up, until blisters raised on Giles fingers and wrist and steam—*or is it smoke?*—rose from his wounds.

Watcher's blood, a sharp wind keened. The pines rustled; sparks shot upward like Guy Fawkes fireworks. *Most rare, and precious.*

"My request must be granted, then," Giles said steadily.

In for long life? Now the fire itself spoke, in sharp, staccato syllables, almost like the *tick-tick-tick* of an old telegraph machine.

"Yes," Giles replied. "But not my own life. That of a young woman."

Buffy Summers. The blade spoke her name like a caress, with tender hunger. *The Slayer.*

"Yes."

All slayers die, Watcher. All mortals do.

"I sense . . . that this birthday may be my slayer's last."

Laughter rolled across the forest. Then it became solid and directional, the timbre off, the sound strange and otherworldly. Giles realized the demon had manifested, and was standing directly behind him. His scalp prickled with alarm, but he did not turn around. The Canon of Krathalal warned that no man may look upon the Dread Ravager of Souls and live.

You want me to spare her then, when her time to join me is come?

The statement alarmed Giles, because it meant that Krathalal assumed he would catch Buffy's soul upon the point of her death. Giles hated the demon then, and all demons, and all the powers of darkness that had pursued Buffy every day and every night since she had been called. He hated that that his charge lived each day knowing that it might be her last.

"I want you to protect her while she lives," Giles explained. "You have that power."

The demon's laughter shook the trees, and the earth. Flames erupted from the magick circle and rose high, and higher still, until they became geysers of searing heat and soaring majesty. The fires were death-colored: gravedirt gray and the dark, mottled green of putrescence. The murky, thick brown of coagulating blood.

That is true. I do have that power.

"Yes, and I . . . I will do anything if you will watch over her."

I shall be her new Watcher, the demon mused. *Making you . . . unnecessary.*

"That's one way of looking at it," Giles bit off.

Hmm. I like this idea. It would be amusing.

"And while you're at it, yes, do spare her on her death."

Your demand has already been spoken. You may not alter it.

Giles hesitated. "Fine," he said. "She'll elude you, at any rate." He was beginning to feel faint. He swayed on his knees as the sweat rose off him. Inside the circle he was getting very, very hot. "I . . . give you my thanks," he added, since the ritual required it.

It's a fair bargain, your life for hers. So, Rupert Giles, remain where you are. Keep bleeding, and burning. Die all night for your slayer. Slowly.

"In return . . . ," Giles began, then gasped as a stab of white-hot pain worked its way through his body, as if the knife had bitten into more of him than the flesh of his palm.

In return I shall guard her, the demon mused. *Until her next birthday . . . if that seems appropriate.*

Her next birthday, Giles thought. *Does he know what just happened? That Dawn discovered the secret of her own existence this very day?*

Does he know that today is Buffy's birthday?

The demon sounded thoughtful. *Birthdays are special occasions, are they not? They mark so much more than the mere passage of time. Particularly for a slayer, who has so few of them.*

I'm dying, Giles thought through a haze of agony. *I'm being cooked alive.*

"You must swear that you will keep watch over her until her next birthday," Giles said. "Otherwise, no deal."

The demon's laughter shattered the forest. Like the

explosions of bombs, every tree within Giles' view burnt into flame. Orange and red whirled and spun like enormous pinwheels, until they collided with one another and thickened into a quaking wall of holocaust.

You seek answers in your book. In your mind. You want to know how to prevent her from suffering so much on each succeeding anniversary of her birth.

"I don't deny it," Giles managed to say.

Perhaps I shall enlighten you.

Rise, Watcher, and walk through the flames. Dare that, and I will seal the bargain.

Shakily, Giles rose. Swaying, he took a step forward, toward the unbelievable blaze. His face was so hot, he thought it must have caught fire. He tried to look down at his body, but all he could see, all that surrounded him, were whirlpooling mixtures of red and orange and yellow.

He took another step, pitching forward, into the tempest of fire.

Her birthdays, Krathalal said. *Let us look at them together.*

And suddenly, he found himself in a time since past. It was Buffy's eighteenth birthday . . . the year of the Cruciamentum.

The year you betrayed her. . . .

"Helpless"

I simply cannot countenance this, Giles wrote furiously in his journal. He sat alone in his office in the murky library of Sunnydale High School, a cup of cold tea at his elbow. His head was throbbing, and he wished himself to be anywhere but in this musty, unloved library, preparing to commit a hateful act. *But there seems to be no way out, either for Buffy or for myself. If I could end it now, I would . . . even if I had to commit murder to do so. That may sound melodramatic, but it would seem a small price to pay indeed, compared to what Buffy will have to endure if I continue on this course. . . .*

Other former lovers might have picnics on hillsides, there to recall fond memories of their faded romance. Bittersweet and gentle, they might lean on an elbow and stare out at the countryside, gesture to a wispy cloud, remark on fields of wildflowers.

Buffy and Angel tried to kill each other.

All in good fun, of course, Buffy thought, as she successfully dodged Angel's renewed attack.

The vampire slayer and the vampire fought in the great room of Angel's art deco mansion, the silent, curved angles fanned like so many sentinels to their battle. Fragrant baguettes and French cheeses were spread on a blanket, along with bottles of water, ripe fruit, and so many vanilla-scented candles that the reflections they cast shimmered against the stonework like the rippling waters of an underground grotto.

Taut, sweaty, and all business, Buffy grabbed Angel's shoulders as hard as she could. *Oh, yeah, no flab there;* he was as solid as a rock and as strong as, well, an immortal vampire who had studied martial arts and who worked out many, many nights of his very long life.

Well, so do I, she thought with a grin as he broke her hold and tried to hoist her over his head. He didn't succeed, and she backed away like a prizefighter, then rushed him and managed a good sidekick to his hip. He grunted, caught her leg, and flipped her.

She landed with the greatest of ease.

Fight, fight, fight. He didn't hold back, and neither did she. That was what made it good, that was why they both enjoyed it. There was no one else Buffy could really go after like this, at least not if she wanted to keep him/her/it around after the battle was over. She would break a human being, and most other vampires never lasted this long.

They both fought in silence, their shadows dancing over the walls and across the ceiling. At times like this, she completely understood Faith's lust for the battle. It felt good to be strong; it was great to have her own power matched against a truly strong adversary. Thanks to seemingly endless training sessions, her muscles and reflexes were both honed to fighting trim; she was lean and aggressive, a slinky cat.

Hah! You're dead meat, tiger!

She spotted an opening in Angel's defenses, brought her knees up hard, flipped him over herself and onto his back. Then she sprang to her feet only a few seconds before Angel recovered and rushed her.

They tussled, and then she sweep-kicked his legs out from under him. He hit the floor again, harder this time, and Buffy thought cockily, *Oooh, another point for the Slayer.*

She grabbed a baguette and rolled—*ha ha, pun, a baguette is a French roll*—over to Angel's flattened body, knelt on his chest, and prepared to deal the deadly, breadly death blow. "Gotcha!" she crowed.

"Right in the heart," Angel agreed, good with her victory. He was totally down with her being all the bad self she could be, gracious in defeat as well as in victory. Never whined when she whomped him, which of late had been more often than usual. 'Course, he was still a little on the raggedy side, having so recently returned from being tortured in the hell dimension and all.

She gave the bread a jaunty toss and said, "Satisfied?"

Then their gazes locked, and Angel's eyes lost their merriment. Instantly they were somewhere else, both of them at the same time, and it was a place of deep connection, of knowing and feeling what the other one was thinking, was feeling.

What each of them was needing, so badly, so hungrily. . .

"I'm not sure that's the word." His voice was low, and she could hear the longing in it because it was echoing in her bloodstream and the pounding of her heart.

Oh, Angel, yes . . .

His body tensed, and as with the other battle they had

just fought, hers responded in kind. They were poised on a brink now; they had just entered the danger zone, and they both knew it. One touch, one caress now, and—

—*and worlds could be lost,* Buffy thought. *We can't. We just can't.*

"Oh, I didn't mean satisfied like—" she blurted, at the same time that Angel said quickly, "No, I wasn't trying to."

"'Cause we're not having satisfaction, in the personal sense," she asserted.

"Of course," Angel replied, but his words were for show, just like hers. He wanted her as much as she wanted him, and she was having just as much trouble keeping any sort of distance between them.

For moving away from him, she should get an award, or some time off for good behavior, or at the very least, some sympathy. Because this was Angel, her soul mate and her love, and she couldn't tempt him, or herself. But she also couldn't pretend that a good fight and a birthday picnic on the floor of his home were enough from him, enough of him.

Troubled, yearning, she said, "I should go. Giles is—"

"Waiting for you. I know." He looked gently sad, as if he was trying not to reveal the depth of his loneliness without her. As the only vampire on earth with a soul, the one being in the world he had ever truly connected with was Buffy. "Am I going to see you this weekend? You probably have plans."

"Birthday, right," she filled in. "Actually, yeah, I do have a thing."

"A thing? A date?" His forehead creased with dismay, and she loved him for it. *Shouldn't love him. Should like him. But I've never been good with rules.* She smiled ruefully. "Nice attempt at casual. Actually, I do have a date. Older man. Very handsome. Likes it when I call him

'Daddy.'" She let her expression go a little dirty-sexy on that last word.

Angel grinned. "Your father." Then the forehead crease returned to its former place of business. "It is your father, right?"

Her smile grew. She had missed her father more than usual of late, maybe because she knew she would be seeing him on her big day. "He's taking me to the ice show. It's great fun. And I could definitely use a little more fun." She gave him a knowing look that translated as, *All work and no play makes Buffy a sloppy Slayer.*

And speaking of the need for more fun . . .

Buffy hiked dutifully to the library, where her Watcher waited with half the Sunnydale Natural History Museum in a cute little box. Actually, it was a big box, and it was Giles's own official Watcher Crystal Kit, obtained from the British division of Mattel for a hundred box tops of sugarless, humorless oat bran cereal. The Watcher was in *mucho* Giles mode, very much nagging her with his tone of voice not to think of ice shows or fun of any sort.

Most of the contents of the box was on the table, a buffet of crystals she had managed to fumble through identifying, and she really, really wished she had an elsewhere to be.

Actually, I do have an elsewhere to be. On patrol. Doing the real slayage stuff.

"And this one?" Giles prodded, dangling a hunk of lavender at her.

Hah. Such a question . . . not. I have earrings made out of this stuff.

"Amethyst."

"Used for?" Giles asked coolly.

He means not as decorative ear objects. "Breath

mint?" *When stumped, go for the lame joke.*

Giles huffed in his huffy British way. "For charm bags, money spells, and cleansing one's aura."

Interesting. As in, not. "Okay, so: How do you know when your aura's dirty? Somebody come by with a finger and write 'wash me' on it?"

He was not amused. "Buffy, I'm aware of your distaste for studying vibratory stones, but as it's part of your training, I'd appreciate your glib-free attention."

"Sorry," she said to the huffmeister. "It's just with Faith on one of her unannounced walkabouts, someone should be out patrolling."

"Faith is not interested in proper training, so I rely on you to keep up with yours."

"I hate being the 'good' one," she grumped. She picked up an interesting-looking crystal and toyed with it.

"And as for patrolling, you'll be out there soon enough. Why so anxious?" Giles asked.

She realized the stone had a certain . . . masculine look to it, and quickly set it down. "Let's just say I've got a lot of energy to burn off." *'Cause that tension around Angel . . .*

"Due time. For the present, if it's not entirely beyond your capabilities, try to concentrate."

She let that snide remark go to the cornfield, where so many others had so boldly gone before. Wished she were there, too.

He placed a large place crystal before her. She sighed heavily, and lazily eyed it. *Note to self: The sooner you get this over with, the sooner you're out of here.*

And that can't be soon enough.

But then again, yay, 'cause sooner or later, all amazingly boring things come to an end.

* * *

She was outta there, and on patrol, and Giles and his boulders were of the recent past. Now she was in the playground, home of much Slayer battle, 'cause sometimes little kids dawdled after dark there, and sometimes big kids did other stuff, making it a sort of watering hole for the night predators of Sunnydale. It was one big circle of death, and she was the kink in the food chain.

The chilly night breeze blew the swings gently back and forth, making them squeak like rusty wind chimes. The whirligig rotated slowly. The moon was big and fat and gorgeous like a disk of crystal whatever.

And she was kicking major vampire butt.

With a good swift body slam, she threw the vamp down the slide. Gravity gave him the ride of his unlife, and he toppled to the ground. Buffy joined him, and the kicks and punches just kept on coming.

"Wow, that was really funny looking," she jibed. "Could you do that again?"

"I'll kill you for that!" the vamp snarled at her.

"For *that*? What were you trying to kill me for before?"

She smashed him in the face with a very cool roundhouse kick, sending him sprawling yet again, this time onto the whirligig. He didn't like it.

She whipped out a stake and got ready for the grand finale.

"Okay, here's the deal," she began, then, *whoosh,* it was like she was the one on the whirligig and it was doing more than rotating slowly. The world spun around way too fast, and she totally lost her focus, so much so that the vamp noticed it and lunged at her.

He threw her to the ground and pinned her; she still had the business end of the stake pointed at his chest, but he grabbed her wrist and twisted it until the stake was pointed at her own chest. The shocking thing was, he accomplished the move almost effortlessly, and now Buffy couldn't seem to stop him as he started pressing it down on her chest. Plus, it *hurt*.

Then he leaned in close and whispered, "Let me know if I'm not doing this right."

Oh, my God, I'm going to die, she thought. *This one stupid vampire is going to pierce me through the heart with my own stake.*

No, I've got to save myself. Use some other fighting strategy . . . only I'm so dizzy, I can hardly think . . . I can't die. That would be bad. . . .

So she headbutted him, way hard, and he rolled off her. His forehead was bleeding, and it was almost like *she* was the vampire, the sight of his blood giving her an anchor to focus on.

As she pushed herself up, she spotted her stake, lying on the ground where it was dropped. She scrambled on all fours to retrieve it. Blood-head guy realized what she was doing and dived at her, like they were both going after the same piece of candy after the *piñata* breaks at a birthday party.

But he was too late. Buffy turned over just with the stake propped up between her fists. The vampire impaled himself on the stake as she held it propped up in her fists.

Screech, poof, the dude was history, and the Slayer was coated with his dust.

She sat up, brushing it off. She was still woozy, and she tried to get over the fact that she had just had a very-near-death experience.

Not loving that, she told herself, *and not loving this weakness.* Experimentally, she opened and closed her fists and felt her arms. Then she got to her feet, checked around for anything else that might qualify as evil, and began to trudge home.

I almost died. She shuddered, even though there was

no breeze, and made her way home. *From one dumb vamp. What if two dumb vamps show up between here and my front porch?*

What is wrong with me?

No answers came, and neither did sleep. She woke up exhausted, got ready for school, made herself eat something, and hurried to join the ranks of America's foot soldiers in the war against ignorance.

She headed for the library, called out for Giles, and realized he hadn't come in yet. *Maybe he's sick, too. Maybe he's at home in bed with a water bottle on his head. Or wherever they go.*

I hope not. I so need him to do the research.

After making sure the "Closed" sign was still placed outside the library's double doors, she rummaged around in the book vault, which doubled as her weapons storage area. There was her bull's-eye, the same one Giles had used when she had arrived in town and they had started training together. *I so sucked back then,* she thought. *My aim was terrible.*

She pinned the large bull's-eye on the wall and gathered up an armful of throwing knives. After a couple of dozen tosses, she had not hit the yellow circle once. Not once. And a number of the knives hadn't been thrown hard enough to pierce the target. They lay on the floor like little silver dead fish.

She was distressed. *I'm worse now than I was then.*

"Bit early in the day," Giles said, as he strode otherwise unannounced into the room.

"Giles," she said anxiously, relieved to see him at last, "something's wrong."

"Wrong?" he echoed.

He followed her gaze to the target, and she looked at what he must be seeing: knives everywhere, sticking out of walls, a bookcase, books—*uh oh, hope he doesn't notice the books part*—and hardly any at all in the target itself.

"Ah," he said, as he took in the carnage. "Perhaps you shouldn't—"

She threw again, and missed again in a spectacular manner.

"—do that anymore," he finished.

"On top of that, I got a bad case of the dizzies last night and almost let a vamp stake me," she told him. "With my own stake!" She tried again, and it was not pretty. "I am way off my game, my game's left the country, it's in Cuernavaca! Giles, what's going on here?"

"Well . . . probably you've got a flu bug or something," he said reasonably. Her total lack of strength and coordination barely seemed to bother him at all.

"On, no," she replied, very, very, very not reassured. "Not sick. I can't get sick. No." She frowned. "My father's coming up to take me to the ice show. We do it every year for my birthday. If I cancel on him, it'll break his heart."

Giles looked a little less like Mr. Data and more like someone who cared about her. "Perhaps you should take it easy for the next forty-eight hours. Forego any more patrolling until you're feeling yourself again."

That sounded too much like admitting defeat. *And am I not a winner?* "No. No, I think I need to spend a little more time training."

This time she hit the front of the glass special collections case, shattering it. "I'm gone."

"Thank you," Giles sang out, and she beat a hasty retreat.

Retreat. Like a loser.

As best she could, Buffy put aside her worry and

concentrated on the good, which was the ice show with her dad. At lunch she met up with Xander, Willow, and Oz. Willow and Oz were cute and couple-y, while Xander was back to his bachelor status. The four of them sat about like seniors should, and she told them all about it, and Xander looked amused.

"An ice show?" he echoed, head cocked, eyebrow arched. "A show performed on ice. And how old are we, again?"

"I saw *Snoopy on Ice* once when I was little," Willow piped up. "My dad took me backstage," she added fondly, and then her expression darkened. "And I got scared and threw up on Woodstock."

"I know you all think it's just a big, dumb, girly thing," Buffy protested, "but it's not. Some of the skaters are Olympic medal winners, and my dad buys me cotton candy, a souvenir program that has pictures every year and . . . okay," she conceded, "it *is* a big, dumb, girly thing, but I love it."

"Not so girly," Oz assured her. "Ice is cool. It's water—but it's not."

Willow smiled adoringly at him, then turned her attention to Buffy. "I think it's sweet, you and your dad have a tradition. 'Specially now that he's not around so much." Then she lowered her voice and advised, "Ixnay on the caramel corn if you're goin' backstage."

Xander added, "Okay, but we're still talking party, right? I mean, some of us relish celebrating the birth of the Buf."

Buffy hesitated. "Maybe it's time to call a moratorium on parties in my honor. They tend to go badly. Monsters crash, people die." She thought about the surprise party the gang had thrown for her last year at the Bronze. They'd snuck in after hours to decorate and arranged a nice cake and other refreshments on the pool table. That was also where she and Miss Calendar had set the box they had stolen from Spike and Dru. Inside had lain the dismembered, still-living arm of the Judge, the evil creature that Spike and Dru were putting back together so he could burn humanity to bits. And of Angel shortly after the discovery, being with her in that special way, and then him going totally evil. . . .

"Eighteen is a big one, Buffy," Willow reminded her. "You can vote now. You can be drafted." She brightened with sudden inspiration. "You can vote *not* to be drafted."

Buffy remained unconvinced. "I think I'll choose to celebrate this one with quiet reflection."

"Where's it written quiet reflection can't be combined with cake and funny hats?" Xander insisted.

Cake and funny hats, Buffy thought, as she walked up the path to the kitchen door of her home. *My friends are so friendly. I am so much lucky Buffy.*

Buffy smelled her mom's awesome spaghetti sauce as she went in and shut the door behind herself.

"Buffy?" Joyce Summers called.

Buffy sang out, "Present." She gave her mom a quick smile and then caught sight of a gigantic arrangement of flowers and Mylar balloons. "Ooh, present," she said happily.

"They're not . . ." Her mom looked uncomfortable. She added, "They're from your father."

The ice show tickets were attached to an envelope. It took Buffy no more time to register the meaning of her not-present. It was supposed to be a consolation prize.

He's not coming.

"His quarterly projections are unraveling, and he can't afford to take off right now. He promises he'll make it up to you. It's all there in the letter."

Buffy plucked the envelope and the tickets off the

bouquet. Her heart felt like it was being dragged through cold mud. She felt stupid for feeling so disappointed, and she tried to tell herself that she was a mature person and that, hey, these things happened.

"If you want, I could ask someone to cover for me at the gallery. I mean, if you want me to take you . . ."

To take me, not to go with me. She doesn't want to go, either, but at least she's trying to do the right thing. Not just blow me off and try to make it okay with a bunch of flowers.

Unseen by her mother, she crumpled the note.

"No," she said firmly. She couldn't explain why she felt embarrassed, but she was. Horribly. And she so did not want to cry in front of her mom. "No, that's not necessary. I was thinking earlier how nice it might be to have a quiet birthday."

And I was wrong.

Approximately eighty-two years before Buffy was born, Sunnydale officially became a town. The name Boca del Infierno was abandoned in favor of Sunnydale, and the only people who remembered the legend about the land sitting on top of hell were the little old ladies who volunteered at the Sunnydale Historical Society. But not even they, with their meticulously kept newspaper clippings and photo albums, noticed how many bizarre and sinister things happened inside the city limits. The populace accepted the feeble explanations put forth by city hall—gas leaks, gangs on PCP, spiked punch—and continued burying their dead in the city's dozen cemeteries. Maybe after a time, the inhabitants got used to the bad vibes, but tourists who might have otherwise come to town for a little getaway, stayed away.

So places like the Sunnydale Arms fell to ruins. ROOMS TO LET, the dilapidated sign invited, added the inducement of BREAKFAST INCLUDED. INQUIRE WITHIN.

But not enough people *had* inquired within. In fact, after a while, no one did. Now the place looked like a haunted house—creepy, mysterious, and spooky. The boardinghouse was large and broken down; overgrown shrubbery choked the last few green blades of an otherwise deceased lawn. The faded sign near the end of what was once a walk dangled from its rotted post, like a worn-out, homeless man who had given up on working for anything, including the hope of one more day on the planet.

Inside the creepy place, past the sparsely furnished anteroom, the windows were being bricked up in preparation for the test. Blair, the man on the ladder, was laying mortar and the final bricks in the frame of a windowsill. Quentin Travers, the senior Watchers Council member on the premises, watched the weary lad and sighed inwardly at the trouble the man was having.

No mason, this one. The resources of the Council have certainly dried up with the years. Time was, we had specialists for every sort of job one could imagine. Now we have to give our juniors the sorts of jobs once reserved for seasoned foot soldiers.

Hobson, the other young Council apprentice, descended the stairs, looking as exhausted as Blair. His work clothes were splattered with mortar.

"How much longer, Hobson?" Quentin asked him.

"Five, maybe six hours, sir," Hobson confessed. The man clearly felt uneasy with manual labor, but he was not about to complain. Quentin gave him high marks for that.

Very English of him. With more like him, we'd not have lost the Empire. But one can hope that we shall win the war that matters more than territories and possessions. We of the Watchers Council of Britain battle for men's souls.

Quentin checked his watch. "Once you've finished,

you and Blair can get some rest," he said, then added, "but sleep in shifts."

Then the low, guttural drone that had served as background noise insisted upon his attention. He followed its course until he stood in front of the heavy wooden crate propped up against the wall, next to a mantelpiece that rather reminded him of an aunt's seaside home in Brighton. The crate, however, was like nothing in the grand lady's parlor; it was old and scarred, the lid padlocked in four places. The hum that emanated from it was unearthly, ungodly.

"We're getting very close," he said appraisingly, taking a step toward the box. "The Slayer's preparation is nearly complete."

Unknown to Travers, the monster inside the box heard every word he spoke.

I am crazy like a fox, the inhabitant thought, humming. *I'm a crazy fox in a box. I was nuts when I was alive and I'm totally whacked out now. And oh man oh man, my slurpy English blood sausage, I'm hungry. Hungry enough to drain a horse.*

But you'll do, Quentin. You'll do just fine.

On the other hand, the Slayer will do even better.

Maybe if I do better with the stones, he'll listen, Buffy hoped, as she sat in the school library and watched Giles set the crystals up like a cheery parade of brave little objects.

"I mean, there's cartoon characters," Buffy piped up. "But they also do pieces from ballets and operas. Brian Boitano doing *Carmen,* it's a life changer. He doesn't actually play Carmen," she added quickly, thinking, *Duh, Summers.* "But a lot of sophisticated people go."

Despite her enthusiasm, the Watcher wasn't catching her drift. She knew, ice shows, not so much a Giles thing, but a girl could hope.

"Yes," he said, still not listening. "I think we should start with the Grounding Crystal again."

"You know, it's usually something families do together." She swallowed nervously. "It's the kind of thing fathers do with their daughters."

His full attention was on the large and sort of pretty Grounding Crystal.

"Now, look very carefully for the tiny flaw at its core," he told her.

"I mean, if someone were free, they'd take their daughter or their student, or their . . . Slayer," she added glumly, because it wasn't looking good for a trip to Dairy Queen, much less to the ice show.

"Hmm? Yes. Buffy. I think we need to concentrate."

She sighed and looked at the crystal.

"Look for the flaw at its center," he urged.

Obediently, she stared. There it was, the flaw, a nugget of cloudiness, a little baby rain cloud that, if life were a cartoon, would be hovering above her blonde Slayer head.

After a minute or so, Giles said softly, "Buffy?"

The Grounding Crystal had done its work. Buffy was unconscious so long as her optic link with the magickal stone was not disturbed. A raven vampire could enter the library and drain the life from his veins—even hers—and she would do nothing to prevent it.

It was time for the dirty business at hand.

Reaching under the table, he picked up his valise and from it plucked the small leather box. Inside glittered the enormous hypodermic needle, filled with yellow liquid. The formula for the poison was over a thousand years old.

Hating himself, he swabbed the inside of her forearm

and injected her with the yellow liquid. He watched her as he shoved the hypo back into the box, and the box back into his valise, and the valise back under the table. As he had been instructed, she neither felt the injection nor reacted to the debilitating chemical reactions that were now taking place inside her body.

Satisfied that all was as it should be, he passed his hand over the Grounding Crystal, breaking her visual connection. She instantly blinked like someone brought out of a hypnotic trance.

"What?" she asked, jerking and blinking. She looked a bit abashed. "Sorry. Must be this flu bug I'm nursing."

"Best take care of that," he said solicitously. "Perhaps we should—"

"Call it a night." She sounded rather dejected, but he was too consumed with his task to understand why. "Good idea. See ya."

As she turned to leave, his warm expression drooped with self-loathing. He felt heartless and ignoble, and he figured that if he had an ounce of self-respect, he would demand an end to this immorality.

Then they'd do it without me, he reminded himself. *At least this way, I can offer her some modicum of protection* . . . .

"Good night," he said.

The next morning, Buffy weaved through the midmorning cattle drive that was the changing of class periods. She felt a little better, and she figured the flu bug was being slayed. Or maybe she was simply enjoying the result of a long-delayed good night's sleep.

Due to the fact that I was so exhausted I could have fallen asleep in the middle of the dance floor at the Bronze. Okay, not. But, anyway . . .

"How goes it with Amy the rat?" she asked the Willster,

who was wearing one of her signature colorful hats. On red-haired Willow, they were cute, funky. But Buffy couldn't imagine any other girl their age who could get away with orange and yellow watch caps topped with pom-poms.

"Good," Willow reported. "She really likes the new exercise wheel. When she runs, her little nose wiggles so happily—"

"I meant, how goes it with changing her back into a human being?" Buffy chided her, ever so gently. Willow's feelings were easily hurt.

"Oh. Still working on it." Willow brightened. "But I did get her the cutest little bell—"

"You don't do that to me!" a guy shouted suddenly.

Shouted at Cordelia Chase, no less. He was hovering menacingly over the beautiful brunette, in a secluded part of the quad.

"I waited for you at the Bronze all night!" he thundered. "What's the story?"

Cordelia glared up—way up—at him. He was a beefy strapper, chunky like a football player or something. "And the big deal is?" Cordy demanded.

He grabbed her arm. Roughly. "You made me look like some kind of dork in front of my posse."

"First of all, 'posse'? *Passé*," Cordelia informed him hotly. "Second, anyone with a teaspoon of brains would know not to take my flirting seriously. Especially with my extenuating circumstance."

"What circumstance?" asked jock-head.

"*Rebound*. Look it up." She turned sharply to leave, and he grabbed her and threw her against a tree. Buffy was instantly transformed from Interested Onlooker Buffy into the Blonde Avenger Buffy.

"I'm not through here," he told Cordelia.

Buffy grabbed his arm. "I beg to differ." Yanked. Yanked again. His arm didn't move. Not one inch, not one centimeter, not one length of a rat's whisker.

He looked down at her like she was a psycho-loony. Buffy tried again with both hands, putting her all into it, and he shoved her aside with barely a glance. She fell hard against the stone bench, her stuffing knocked out, and tumbled hard to the ground.

Willow rushed to her side while Cordelia absorbed what had just happened. With a grunt of total fury, she started socking the jerk anywhere she could reach, mostly on his chest and shoulders.

"What is wrong with you?" she shrieked as the guy backed off. She pursued, really whamming him.

"The chick started it," he insisted defensively.

That infuriated Cordelia even more, and she pumped up the volume, doing a full Rocky Balboa on his person. He went into *uber*-retreat mode, head cradled between his elbows.

Willow asked Buffy, "Are you okay?"

Buffy stared wordlessly up at her, so very not.

Eventually Buffy merged with the traffic in the school hall, putting on the turbo charge when she saw Giles. She said, "Okay, I just got swatted down by some no-neck and rescued by *Cordelia*. What the hell is happening, Giles?"

"All right, calm yourself," he said calmly.

Her eyes practically spun, she was so beyond calm. "Are you getting the big picture here? I have no strength! I have no coordination. I threw knives like . . . like . . ."

"A girl?" he asked.

Help me! she pleaded with her eyes.

"Look, Buffy, I assure you, given time, we'll get to the bottom of whatever's causing this . . . anomaly."

So that means he thinks it'll go away. She kept the eyes big, but it required no effort on her part, really. She was scared to death. And this "wait and see" attitude was so unlike Research Man that it offered little comfort.

"Promise me?"

"Yes. I give you my word."

Mildly comforted . . . *but only mildly, and only 'cause it's Giles,* she headed off to her next class.

As Giles sat in the hellish prison that had once been the ruins of the Sunnydale Arms, he himself was not at all comforted.

The dilapidated parlor offered dreary, tattered furnishings and bricked-up entrances and exits. No one got in, no one got out . . . unless the Council permitted it.

It was absurd that Giles's superior, Quentin Travers, had offered him tea. It was even more absurd that he had accepted it. That they should be mired in the courtesies when they were discussing the possibility of Buffy's death revolted him down to the soles of his shoes.

"You're having doubts," Quentin said unnecessarily. "The Cruciamentum is not easy. For Slayer or Watcher. But it's been done this way for a dozen centuries, whenever a slayer turns eighteen. It's a time-honored rite of passage."

"It's an antiquate exercise in cruelty," Giles objected. To lock her in this tomb, weakened, defenseless, to unleash *that* on her—"

He tried to keep his tone emphatic without losing his temper. "If any one of the Council still had actual contact with a slayer, they'd see. But *I'm* the one in the thick of it."

"Which is why you're not qualified to make this decision. You're too close," Travers pointed out, also emphatic, and much further from the point of losing his temper. But why shouldn't he be? He was supremely detached from Giles's concerns. His focus was ensuring that the test be carried out fairly and honestly, not on worrying that Buffy might fail it . . . by dying.

"Not true," Giles insisted.

"I'm sorry." Quentin did look perhaps a tiny bit sympathetic after all. "A slayer must be more than physical prowess. She must have cunning, imagination, a confidence derived from self-reliance. Believe me, once this is all over, your Buffy will be stronger for it."

"Or she'll dead for it," Giles snapped.

He rose and made his way to the front hallway. Quentin accompanied him, looking pleased at the sight of a young man adjusting a large spring mechanism at the front door.

"Rupert," Quentin began, and Giles looked at him. "If this girl is everything you say, then you've nothing to worry about."

Giles nodded slightly—*damn public school manners*—and left, tight-lipped and silent, and very, very worried.

Ah, damn, Quentin thought. *Rupert's always been something of an unknown quantity in Council dealings. I'm certain he doesn't realize that I've pled his case on a number of occasions, and they've been on the verge of sacking him ever since Buffy Summers moved here. I'm the best friend he has in London. But I know what he thinks of me, and of this test.*

I wish I had the luxury of taking that into account, but I most certainly do not.

Hobson said to him, "Sir, if you can spare me for a short spell, I'll need to make a run to the hardware store. I just need some—"

A bloodcurdling, feral shriek cut him off. Quentin and Hobson traded looks. Blair appeared, his face pale and his demeanor that of a terribly frightened man.

Quentin said brusquely, "Take care of it."

The trio made their way back to the room with the

large crate. Blair removed a ring of keys from his pocket and began to unlock the numerous padlocks. Quentin stood by, wielding a large fire ax as the two younger Council members pried open the crate's lid.

The towering monster inside was swaddled in a strait-jacket. He was a vampire, quite insane, with a metal band strapped across his forehead and bolted into the wood on either side to immobilize his head. His fangs were long and extremely pointed. His eyes were clenched shut, partly because of vampiric light sensitivity, Quentin assumed, but more likely from searing pain. He was given to incapacitating headaches—the same chronic condition that had tormented him as a human being . . . if Zackary Kralik could ever have been said to have been a human being.

His eyes snapped open. Hobson and Blair were rooted to the spot, horrified by his gaze.

"Come on, come on," Quentin urged.

Blair attended to one of two prescription bottles on the mantel. He placed two pills into an enormously long spoon as the others watched. Standing as far away as he could manage, Blair lifted the wand to Kralik's mouth. The vampire was oblivious, too caught up in his pain to realize that relief lay within his grasp.

"Kralik," Blair said unsteadily. "Your pills. Open your mouth."

Kralik complied. His fangs glistened with saliva, and Quentin felt a frisson of fear. Kralik was the most vicious vampire the Council could acquire, saved for just this occasion. It had been a long, hard job to keep watch over him, but they had done so. No matter the outcome of the Cruciamentum, Quentin was going to recommend his termination. It was too risky to keep him alive any longer.

Hobson approached with a pair of tongs that held a glass of water. Standing to the side, he brought the glass to the vampire's mouth and poured the water in. Kralik drank voraciously, water dribbling down his chin.

"That's enough. Close it up," Quentin ordered.

The young men rushed to do it, closing the lid and reattaching the locks. No one wanted to see Kralik. No one wanted to be in the same room with him.

But we're Council, Quentin thought with satisfaction. *We do what must be done.*

The Scooby gang was ensconced in the school library, aka Slayage Central, doing what they hated best—combing through stacks and stacks of books about monsters, vampires, and the assorted death stylings of various other creatures of darkness. The reading was not of the funnest, except for Willow, who had the weird notion that researching arcane facts about ooga-booga stuff was funner than just about anything in the world, possible exception being smoochies with Oz.

Xander, Cordelia-less, and thus far into the rebound, still not so into the book learnin', was grateful beyond his fragile years when Willow perked up and crowed, "Aha! A curse on slayers!"

Yes, Xander cheered. *Free at last, thank God, I'm—*

"Oh, no, wait." Willow made a sorry face. "It's lawyers."

Darn. In desperation, he trotted out some double-talk designed to get him out of the library and into the real world.

"Maybe we're on the wrong track with the spells, curses, and whammies. Maybe what we should be looking for is something like Slayer kryptonite."

"Faulty metaphor," Oz noted. "Kryptonite kills."

"You're assuming I meant green kryptonite," Xander said, with the confidence of a comic book geek extraordinaire. "I was referring, of course, to red kryptonite, which drains Superman of his powers."

"Wrong." Oz gave his head a shake. "Gold kryptonite's the power-sucker. Red kryptonite's the one that mutates Superman into some sort of weird—"

"—Guys," Buffy interrupted testily, gesturing to both her Buffiness and the books. "Reality?"

That shut them down, but Xander was not out. He had not spent half his life reading comics only to be dissed by disinformation from a guy in a band, for heaven's sake.

Willow and Buffy moved to a more rarefied corner of the library, maybe for privacy. But Xander heard every word.

"Buffy," Willow said soothingly, "I know you're definitely, without a doubt, going to get your powers back."

"Thanks, Will," Buffy said gratefully.

"But . . . what if you don't?" Willow asked.

Jeez, Will, Xander thought, listening even harder.

"Okay." Buffy took a breath. "If I don't get my powers back, I . . . don't. I'll deal. There's a whole lot of good sides to it."

"Actually," Willow said, "it could really open up—"

But that thread got snipped the second Giles walked into the library.

Buffy headed him off at the middle of the floor and said, "Did you find out . . . anything?"

The G-man took a big G-breath. "No. Not yet."

Huh, Xander thought. *Not the usual thing for him, acting like she's buggin' with a big-ass question like that. Maybe he's got acute Watcher-waster disease, only instead of the losing the ability to punch and slash like the Buffster, his vast powers of sarcasm and sardonic British humor will mysteriously disappear.*

Then I, and I alone, will rule as king of the witty retort.

Muwahaha.

* * *

Blair didn't think he'd fallen asleep; how could anyone sleep through Kralik's infernal screaming? But suddenly he bolted awake, in fear for his life; and realized that it was only Hobson, entering the room.

"It's your shift," Hobson announced, rather more forcefully than was necessary, as if he was afraid that Blair might refuse.

Blair left the room as Hobson lay down, putting the pillow over his head.

It won't work, Blair thought grimly. *Nothing keeps those sounds out.*

He padded down the hall, unable to hear his own footfalls over the shrieks of the frenzied creature. He opened up Kralik's box and took a look; the vampire appeared to be in excruciating pain. Blair wasn't precisely sure what was wrong with him, but he knew that he had to have his pills on a rigid schedule.

I should withhold them, pay him back for all the screaming, Blair thought.

But he wasn't that sort of man, and he had an obligation to fulfill. So he left Kralik with his straitjacket on and his head bolted to the back of the box, and padded into the kitchen. Kralik screamed as if with desperate agony, prodding Blair into shouting back nervously, "It's coming!"

The glass filled, he got the medication out as Kralik shouted, "Pills!" Blair placed them at the end of the administering device; hanging as far back as he could manage, he offered it to the stricken vampire. But Kralik now refused them, like a petulant infant.

"Take them," Blair said impatiently.

"Pills!" Kralik bellowed.

"They're right in front of you." Blair moved the wand so that Kralik could focus on it.

"Where?"

Exhausted, frightened, and quite eager to be done

with the odious task before him, Blair moved slightly closer to the vampire.

"Here," Blair told him.

Kralik said, "Can't see . . . can't reach . . ."

Blair came closer still. "Open your ey—"

Without a moment's warning, Kralik's hand gripped Blair's throat. He felt his eyes bulging as Kralik lifted him off the ground.

He's got loose somehow! Blair thought wildly. *He worked his way out of his jacket! He tricked me!*

He kicked in the air, absolutely wild to save himself. Kralik said in hushed, gleeful voice, "Shhh . . . everything's okay now."

Blair's last thought was of his aunt's seaside home, and of his mother standing at the windowpane, watching a sudden downpour.

"No, dear, you can't go out," she was saying to her young son, still in short pants. "You'll catch your death."

Oh, my God, my death has caught me.

The bite to his neck was excruciating.

As her world had careened further and further out of control, Angel's mansion had become the warmest, safest place Buffy knew. Despite the obvious temptations and the dangers—Angel so close and yet so untouchable—she could almost relax. Many times in the past, she had taken refuge in his arms; tonight, she found sanctuary in his presence, and that was enough. Almost.

And this is nice, Buffy thought, savoring the moments that made up her birthday celebration. *A fire that flickers on Angel's craggy hero-face and a present for me in my lap.*

She suspected it was a book, or maybe a diary . . . maybe Angel's diary, if he kept one, and he had wrapped it in cloth and tied it with twine. It was both kind of homespun and romantic at the same time.

She unwrapped it—*book, after all*—and looked at the cover. *Browning's Sonnets.* She had no idea who Browning was, but she didn't let on. Instead, she lifted the front cover and read his one-word inscription: ALWAYS.

Buffy was touched; she smiled gently as she closed the book and said, "Angel, thank you. It's beautiful."

Angel frowned slightly, looking unsure. "You really like it?"

Busted, she thought. Trying for more enthusiasm, she leafed through the book. "Of course I do. It's thoughtful and sweet and, uh, full of neat words to learn and say, like 'wilt' and 'henceforth' . . ." *And when will I ever learn to keep my mouth shut if all that's gonna come out of it is useful words and expressions in Stupidese?*

"Then why did you seem more excited last year when you got a severed arm in a box?" His tone was kind, and it was moments like these that reminded Buffy of how very, very old Angel actually was.

She decided to share; she needed to share with him. After all, he was Angel and that meant . . . that he was here, for her, in a way that no one else could ever be.

"It's just . . . suddenly there's this chance that my calling could be a wrong number. I guess it's freaking me out a little."

"That's understandable," he replied.

"Angel, what if I have lost my powers?" She searched his face.

"You lived a long time without them. You can do it again."

"I guess." She paused, unconvinced. "But what if I can't? I've seen too much now. I know what goes bump in the night. Not being able to fight it . . . what if I just hide under my bed, all scared and helpless?"

She had a worse thought. "Or what if I just get pathetic? Hanging out at the 'Old Slayers' Home' talking people's ears off about my glory days? Showing them Mr. Pointy, the stake I had bronzed?"

Angel moved to her, speaking soothingly. "Buffy, you'd couldn't be helpless or boring, not even if you tried."

She was not gentled. "Oh, don't be so sure. Before I became the Slayer I was . . . well, I don't want to say shallow, but . . . let's just say a certain person who shall remain nameless, let's call her 'Spordelia,' looked like a classical philosopher next to me. "

Then she took a breath and took the plunge, speaking the words she feared most: "Angel, if I'm not the Slayer, what do I have to offer? What do I do?" Lowering her voice, she added, "Why would you like me?"

To her relief, he didn't start speaking over her, trivializing her concerns with empty words like 'completely acceptable just the way you are.'" Instead, he said, very quietly, "I saw you before you became the Slayer."

Buffy was stunned. "What?"

"I watched you," he said. "I saw you called. It was a bright afternoon out in front of your school. You walked down the steps, and I loved you."

"Why?" she asked, bewildered.

"Because I could see your heart. You held it before you for everyone to see, and I worried that it would be bruised or torn. More than anything in my life I wanted to keep it safe, to warm it with my own."

She folded into his arms, comforted, loved.

"That's beautiful," she breathed. And then, as she thought about it a moment longer, she added, "Or, taken literally, incredibly gross."

And the wonderful thing was that even as Angel replied, "I was just thinking that too," that just made him seem all the more *hers*. All the more, *here*.

"Mmm, mmm," the vampire Zackary Kralik hummed to himself. *Nice place I got here. Add some more splattered blood, a few humans hanging upside down and screaming for their lives, and it'll be home. And the room service is finger-lickin', mmm, mmm good. Not as good as Mom used to be, but what is?*

He let the warm blood trickle down the back of his throat. Then the dead face of Watcher Blair morphed as a demon took up shop and the corpse's eyes snapped open. He got to his feet as Kralik watched approvingly.

"You're up. I was afraid I drained you too much. I do that sometimes." *And sometimes it's even by accident.*

His new minion wordlessly picked up the same ax that devil Quentin Travers had held when he'd last been here.

Kralik hummed some more, turning the notes of a long-lost melody over and over as he tried to catch the tune. Sometimes he could actually see music; he could visualize the notes dripping like pieces of flesh impaled on butcher paper as clearly as if he were still back at the beginning, murdering people in his old hometown for simple thrills and financial gain.

"Ever have a tune you can't get out of your head?" he asked Blair. "Keep playing over and over? Drives me nuts."

The joke was lost on Blair, but that was all right. He was laying into the bracket that held Kralik's head in place. It didn't take long, and within seconds Kralik was finally, blessedly free, stepping out of that damn box and letting his straitjacket slip to the floor.

"Thank you," he said. "That's much better." He turned his head, cracking his neck. "It's a game, you know. We're not going to play by their rules . . .but that doesn't mean we're not going to play." He chuckled. "Why don't you call in your friend . . . and we'll discuss it over dinner?"

* * *

I'll no longer be a party to this, Giles wrote in his journal. He looked up from the nearly blank page and realized he'd been having an imagined conversation with Quentin Travers ever since the man had left the library. Rather than writing, he'd spun a fantasy scene in which he'd managed to say all the things he wished he'd thought of while his superior was still present.

He sighed. He'd pretty much given up the practice since Jenny's death . . . so many of the conversations he'd planned to have with her had never happened.

Ah, Jenny . . .

His heart sank, and he tapped the pen to the page, much as one might tap one's fingers. Then, his features hardening with resolve, he laid down the pen.

Enough.

He would not make the mistake of doing too little too late for another person he cared about. He would tell Quentin in no uncertain terms that the Cruciamentum was not going to proceed. Buffy's distress had sorely tested him, but the looks of confusion and hurt on her face as he repeatedly dodged her appeals for help were too much for him to take.

He drove to the Sunnydale Arms and got out of his Citroën. He stood for a moment taking the measure of the abominable place, asking himself what he planned to do if Quentin refused to listen to reason. Find Buffy and tell her, of course. And then . . . ?

Time enough to decide that later, he reminded himself as he walked down the path toward the front door. The place was eerily silent. No hammers, no voices. Against the moon, the Sunnydale Arms stood silent as a tomb.

The only sound was the crunch of his shoes on some gravel; he took care to move quietly as he kept listening for signs of life. *Have they begun it already?*

Has she already lost?

He pushed open the door and stood on the threshold. "Quentin?"

No answer.

Against his instincts, he walked into the place. The place smelled odd, as if the old boards of the walls had been rearranged, allowing mold and decay to permeate the atmosphere. It was the smell of mausoleums and coffins. It was the smell of something long dead, something so old, it had stopped rotting long ago.

He peered into the parlor to find it empty. Kralik's crate stood with its lid firmly closed, its contents blessedly silent.

The monster must be sleeping. Or whatever passes for sleeping.

He looked round, increasingly uneasy by the stillness. Finding no one about, he crossed to the staircase and began to ascend, calling out, "Hello? Quentin? Hob—"

There was something tacky on the banister. He held his hand up to the light.

It was blood. A great deal of it.

Something's gone horribly wrong.

A chill ran through him; he quickly glanced up to the top landing, then at the crate. Squinting in the dim light, he noticed for the first time the unlocked padlocks and open latchings.

Oh, my God.

For a moment he literally couldn't think. Then his eyes widened as terror seeped into them. Instinctively, he backed away from the crate, then broke one of the staircase's vertical posts. It would make a serviceable stake.

He walked steadily but carefully to the crate, took hold of the lid, and ripped it open.

It was empty—just shattered brackets, a torn strait-jacket, and splintered wood.

And more blood. God, a trail of it.

It led to a closed door to the right of the mantelpiece. Crossing to it, he turned the knob and opened the door slowly, his stake poised and ready. He flicked on the light.

There was blood, everywhere. Blood, streaked and splattered all over the wall and the door. One bloody arm, a human arm, was visible in the light; he moved slightly, saw the rest of the body, and bolted.

He pulled out his handkerchief and gagged.

Kralik's gone, he realized.

He's gone after Buffy.

Giles raced from the house.

He had never moved faster in his life.

The moon shone through clouds, lighting Buffy's way, and she walked beneath a burnt-out streetlamp. Noises carried on in the night air, making her jumpy in a way she could never recall, ever in her life. Not even when she had been an airhead back at Hemery, more wor-ried about getting caught for 'lifting lipsticks than finding a monster at her back.

Gathering her coat around herself, the Slayer felt small and alone as she trudged down the wet street. *And, okay, use the word, "helpless."* She wasn't used to it, and she hated it.

Up the street, two bulky guys loitered beside a car, and they both gave her a lewd once-over as she drew near. Her spine stiffened, and a thrill of nervousness skittered like ice-cold fingers up and down her spine. Jumping at shadows wasn't fun, but negotiating for personal space was definitely worse.

As she passed the two guys, one called out, "Hey, sweet girl. How much for a lap dance for me and my buddy?"

He chuckled, and his buddy joined in. Buffy steeled her jaw. Her flight-or-fight reflex prompted her to pause. For one quick moment, she considered kicking their butts, and then, with total frustration, realized that she had to let it go. Give them a pass, let them bully her. She couldn't hope to take them out in her weakened condition.

I hate this. Is this how all the other girls feel? 'Cause it sucks.

Their laughter followed her as she moved away from them. "Walk me home, Angel?" she mocked, repeating the last words of her good night with him. "No. I'm fine. I can take care of myself."

Summers, you moron.

She walked a few more steps, alert to the sounds of night—crickets, the surf of the occasional passing vehicle, the distant bark of a dog. She heard her own footsteps. There were no others, and that soothed her somewhat.

Then she heard a very weird sound. It took her a moment to realize that it was humming—low, guttural, and tuneless—and she wondered if the two guys had followed her. Unnerved, she looked around, behind herself. It was not the no-necks, and she kept her vigilance, so not loving her impersonation of a hundred chicks in a hundred horror movies, drifting along in all her blonde stupidity, a lovely bit of smuckbait that the audience could watch get chomped by the ever-craftier chainsaw-wielding psycho.

Only, no movie. Reality. Mine.

"Hummers," she said in a loud voice. "Big turnoff. I like guys who can remember the lyrics."

With that bit of bravado, she whirled around to face down her stalker. And gasped.

She stood smack up against a tall, crazed-looking

vampire, who grinned evilly down at her and said, "Wish I could, but my mind's not what it used to be."

Buffy tried to pull away, but the vampire grabbed the sleeve of her coat. Instinctively, she hit him in the face. Twice. He didn't register it at all. Her mind flashed back to Cordelia's human predator, who had thrown Buffy against the stone bench; and then to the vampire in the playground, the one who had almost taken her out. This vamp was bigger and scarier; the air of menace surrounding him was palpable. She was in huge trouble.

Her terror building, the Slayer whimpered, "Let me go."

"Didn't say 'please,'" he said, mocking her. He pulled her closer, fangs bared, and she was so terrified, she could barely think.

Gotta do something, save myself. Gotta act. I'm the Slayer.

Oh, God, I'm Buffy Anne Summers and I'm only eighteen and don't want to die like this, alone and helpless and a victim.

Then her sleeve slipped off her arm. She used the opportunity to slip out of her coat, then retreated, only to find another vampire blocking her way. "Get off me!" she screamed.

She took off in the opposite direction, running for her life, only she wasn't running like the Slayer, she was running like someone who cut P.E. every other day and smoked two packs a day. Her lungs burned, and she wheezed, arms and legs flailing so badly, she knew would fall down hard and smack her face against the street if she lost her footing.

Almost casually, as if her head start were negligible, the taller of the two vampires gestured with his head and the second one raced after her.

She looked around, desperately, for a way to safety,

then spotted a high, chain-link fence and made for it. "Help me, please!" she shouted.

She lunged for the fence, feeling the uneven, cold metal biting into her fingers as she clung to it, unable to use her leaping ability to clear it. Frantically she tried to climb it, but she didn't have nearly enough strength. Her muscles were loose and unresponsive; she was clumsy and terribly weak. There was no way she could get over this fence, no other way to run.

Then she noticed a small hole in the webbing in front of her, dropped down, and awkwardly pushed herself through. The jagged-cut links scratched her face and arms, but she had no time to register the pain—the minion vamp was on her, grabbing her leg. The vamp was powerful, its grip vise-like.

She kicked and struggled, screaming, straining to get through the hole; the vampire yanked and pulled, and she thought once again that she was going to die. Then, miraculously, she got through, got free, and lumbered to her feet.

Headlights bathed her as she got her bearings; it was an oncoming car, and Buffy waved her arms, shouting at it. "Stop! Please!" she cried. "I need—"

But the car didn't slow. In fact, it almost mowed her down.

"Stop!" she pleaded, dodging out of the way.

She looked back at the face to see the vampire scaling it. She screamed and turned to run, failing to notice the lights from another oncoming car, heading straight for her.

Too late to jump out of the way, Buffy braced to be hit. At the last instant, the car swerved to her right and screeched to a halt. The passenger door swung open.

It was Giles, behind the wheel of his Citroën.

"Hurry!" he barked.

She got in, and Giles put the pedal to the metal even before she got the door closed; then she realized the vampire was at the door, pulling on it. Buffy finally managed to kick him off. He hit the road and rolled for a few feet.

But like all immortal beings, he pulled himself back up. But Giles had successfully widened the distance between the vamp and the car, and Buffy turned around.

The other vampire, the taller, crazy one, stood in the center of the road, wrapped in her sweater.

It's okay, Buffy told herself. *I'm safe.*

My Watcher was watching out for me.

This is going to be one of most difficult conversations of my life, Giles thought as he and Buffy sat in the school library. *Made no easier by how relieved Buffy was to see me. She thought of me as her grand rescuer when I . . . I have so betrayed her.*

He had wrapped her in a blanket. She had waved off his offer of tea, too upset to think about trifles. She was reliving her attack, much as normal people do, her mind trying to wrap around the dangerous situation and find some way to undo the damage that had been done her. But she had it all wrong: the two vampires, while deadly, were not as evil as the man standing before her: he, Rupert Giles. A man with a proven capacity to deal with the darkness and come out ahead.

"When I hit him, it felt like my arm was broken. It hurt so *much.* Giles . . . I can't be . . . just a person. I can't be helpless like that." Her eyes were huge. "We have to find out what's happening to me."

There is nothing I can tell her except the truth, he thought. *And the truth is that I'm a deceitful coward who had nearly gotten her killed at least two times that I know of, since Quentin Travers brought the Inquisition to this town.*

For a moment he was tempted to go into his office, retrieve his journal, and let her read what essentially amounted to his written confession of the entire affair. But that would be harder on her—and worse, easier on him. He deserved to suffer for what he had done.

Wordlessly, numb from head to toe, he fetched the leather case and placed it in front of her, opening it to reveal the hypo and a vial of pale yellow liquid.

"It's an organic compound of muscle relaxants, adrenal suppressers—" he took a breath— "The effect is temporary. You'll be yourself again in a few days."

He spoke slowly, wanting to ensure that he told her all of it, that he left nothing out from fear that she would never, ever be able to forgive him. Even if it cost him her respect and love, she would know what he had done to her.

Buffy extended a quivering hand, taking the box and staring at it with growing revulsion. She was clearly in a stunned haze, not quite comprehending the enormity of his role in her misery. "You . . . ," she rasped.

Giles swallowed hard. "It's a test, Buffy." He couldn't get the gentleness out of his voice. He so wanted to make things right again. He didn't know how, but he had to. "It's given to a slayer when she reaches—*if* she reaches—her eighteenth birthday."

He paused for her reaction. She simply continued to stare at the hypo. "The Slayer is disabled, then entrapped with a vampire foe whom she's to defeat in order to pass." He began to pace. He couldn't stand her paralysis, her absolutely inability to absorb what he was telling her.

"The vampire you were to face has escaped. His name is Zackary Kralik. As a human, he'd murdered, tortured, more than a dozen young women before being committed to a sanitarium for the criminally insane."

He ducked just in time as the leather box went flying

at his head. The hypo and vial of potion shattered against a bookcase.

He looked over at Buffy, who was shaking from head to toe, though with rage more than shock.

With hatred.

Oh, Buffy . . . don't hate me . . . forever.

"You bastard! All this time, you saw what it was doing to me. All this time, and you didn't say a *word!*"

"I wanted to . . ." The words were entirely inadequate, indefensible.

"Liar!" she shrieked.

"In matters of tradition and protocol, I must answer to the Council." As he spoke, his poor girl buried her face in her hands. "My role in this was very specific. I was to administer the injections, then direct you to the old boardinghouse on Prescott Lane. . . ."

"I can't . . . I can't hear this," she managed.

"Buffy, please." He couldn't hear it, either. What had he been thinking? How could he have done it?

"Who are you?" she asked brokenly. "How could you do this to me?"

He reached for her, ready to do anything to close the chasm between them. "I'm deeply sorry, Buffy. You have to understand—"

She spoke through clenched teeth. *"If you touch me, I'll kill you."*

"You have to listen to me," he said. "Because I have told you this, the test is invalidated. You'll be safe. I promise." His voice caught. "Whatever I have to do, to deal with Kralik and to win back your trust—"

"You stuck a needle in me. You poisoned me," she said in a low, angry voice.

"What's going on?" a voice chirped from the doorway.

It was Cordelia, who entered, looked at each of them

in turn, assessing the gravity of the situation, and groaned. "Oh, god. Is the world ending? I have to research a paper on Bosnia for tomorrow, but if the world's ending I'm not gonna bother."

Buffy started out of the library.

"Buffy, you can't walk home alone," Giles called after her. "It isn't safe."

He moved toward her, and she turned, facing him down with bitter loathing on her face. She looked so young, and utterly abandoned. He hated himself then.

"I don't know you," she spat at him.

"Did someone take her memory?" Cordelia asked innocently. She turned to Buffy, gesturing toward Giles. "He's Giles. Ji-yills. He hangs out here a lot."

Buffy's face never changed as she said, "Cordelia, could you please drive me home?"

Cordelia was clearly taken aback by the request, but she asked no questions. She simply said, "Sure," and Giles was grateful for the discovery that Cordelia was, after all was said and done, a friend to Buffy.

Buffy continued walking out. Cordelia followed, sighing over her shoulder to Giles. "But if the world doesn't end, I'm gonna need a note."

Joyce Summers had bills to pay. *I always have bills to pay,* she thought, *but I'm a gal of the nineties—single working mom, small portfolio to pay for college if Buffy gets to go, make the mortgage, and have some left over for Cherry Garcia ice cream.*

As she marked down the amount of her last oil change, she cocked her head. There was a strange sound outside. It sounded like moaning, or crying.

On the alert, she went to the front door and opened it.

Someone was balled in a fetal position at the front of the porch.

Her stomach clutched. *That's Buffy's coat.*

"Buffy?"

Every mom-sense she possessed went into hyper-drive as she hurried to her daughter and touched her arm.

The figure rolled over. It wasn't Buffy. It was a vampire, with a mean, feral smile and eyes that spun with madness.

It said to her, in a lazy, crazy way, "Mother?"

Cordelia gave Buffy a ride home. No way would Buffy Summers ever sit in a car with Rupert Giles again.

The decision brought with it enormous pain. Or something worse than pain.

There are no words that describe how I feel, Buffy thought as she let herself into the silent kitchen. Her gaze lighted on the flower arrangement her father had sent her. Light-headed, heart sick, she swept the flowers into the trash, where they belonged.

Both of them. Giles and Dad.

She walked on through, and that was when she noticed that the front door was ajar. *And the house is too quiet.* Her training took over, crowding out fear as she started scanning for signs of a struggle, or for an intruder. *And for my mom.*

There was something small and square taped to the door. Buffy crossed to it.

Then the fear came, waves and waves of it that threatened to overwhelm her. The Polaroid picture was of her mother, her eyes huge with terror, and the tall vampire who had attacked Buffy earlier with his hand around her throat. Buffy blanched and turned the picture over. Written in marker, across the backing:

COME.

That one word became her entire world. To maintain her self-control, she kept her mind filled with it as she went upstairs and changed her clothes. Stifling her panic, she was as grim-faced as any warrior, dressing for battle in a pair of overalls and a long-sleeved top. With steady hands, she put her hair back. Resolved and focused, she threw her weapons bag on the bed and stocked it. Stakes, crosses, crossbow. Holy water in her overall pocket. Another cross.

Done, she grabbed the handle and prepared to hoist the bag off the bed. It was amazingly heavy. *Of course. My strength's still diminished.*

But the heft of the bag did not deter her. With renewed effort, she managed to lug the thing out of her bedroom.

Assisted by a second vampire, the monster had dragged Joyce through the streets of Sunnydale. As on most evenings, there were few people out, and none of them realized that the woman being held so closely by her tall companion was a kidnapping victim in the clutches of a walking nightmare.

Hope flared once when a car going the other way slowed and the driver—a young man—peered through the window at Joyce and the monster. Joyce tried to cry out, but the vampire murmured, "Careful, careful," and squeezed her shoulder so hard she thought it would snap.

The car drove on, and Joyce despaired.

Buffy will find me, she told herself. But she knew that was exactly what this . . . *thing* wanted.

Then the vampire muttered, "Almost there," and hit her so hard that Joyce tumbled into darkness and fell limp in his embrace.

When Joyce came to, she was surrounded by the dimmest possible light. Her head throbbing, she sat bound to a chair, her mouth gagged, in the middle of a dank, empty cellar. It stank of filth and rotten meat, and the air was thick and greasy. Joyce fought to keep her panic from overwhelming her, but it was almost impossible.

"Mother," her captor cooed from the shadows. "May I call you Mother?"

Terrified, she tried to find him in the darkness. Her heart pounded so hard, she couldn't hear herself breathe. Then she realized she was holding her breath and tried to exhale. She couldn't.

I'm losing it, she thought. *I can't lose it. I have to save myself. But Buffy will come for me. No, I don't want her to come here. I want her to stay away, to be safe.*

But I don't want to die. . . .

The Polaroid camera flashed, blinding her. He had already taken dozens of pictures of her. Maybe hundreds by now.

"My own mother was a person with no self-respect of her own," he explained calmly, "so she tried to take mine. Ten years old and she had the scissors; you wouldn't *believe* what she did with those—"

Flash! Joyce cringed from the assault on her dilated pupils.

"But she's dead to me now." He chuckled, and the sound was like fingernails on a blackboard. "Mostly 'cause I killed and ate her."

Oh, no, no, Joyce thought wildly; *please don't do that to me. Just disappear; just be a bad dream and let me wake up in Los Angeles, with my husband beside me and my little girl padding in—let Buffy be six again, or seven—in the jammies with the pink-and-yellow kittens on them, asking for waffles. Make it all go away, please. . . .*

With a supreme act of will, she refocused her attention. She spotted a pitcher of water and a glass on a stool, and hoped they were for her. Because if they were, then he would have to untie the gag. And if he did that, maybe she would be able to breathe.

Then she saw a prescription bottle and some pills in it, and her hopes transformed into yet more fear.

"But it's okay," he assured her. "Because I know I won't be alone much longer. I'll have your daughter. I won't kill her. I'll make her like *me*. Different. She'll go to sleep and when she wakes up—" He paused for effect— "your face will be the first thing she eats."

He came in close, and she reared in fright. "I have a problem with mothers," he confessed lightly. "I'm aware of that."

Joyce, terrified beyond words, violently and vainly struggled.

Oh, my God, oh, my God . . .

The Sunnydale Arms was a nightmare house not come to life at all; it was dead and it was possessed, and Buffy Summers began to tremble as she moved slowly into the dark space. Slabs of shadow choked off starlight and moonlight as she examined her surroundings as best she could.

I'm scared, she thought miserably. *I'm weak and I'm tired and I'm . . .*

And then it came to her:
I am still the Chosen One.
I am the Slayer.

From somewhere deep inside herself, that thought burned like an ember; as she let herself feel it, it grew into a flame. *Whatever the reason that I got Called, it's still valid. It's still real. The Slayer is who I am, what I am, even if the Council tries to take it from me. They can't. They didn't give it to me in the first place.*

Renewed, she knelt down and stuck a stake in the doorway to keep the door slightly propped open as she closed it on the makeshift doorstop. She pulled out a loaded crossbow—her favorite weapon, compact and lethal.

Like me. Like I still am.

I can do this. For my mom, I can do anything.

Moving stealthily, like an assassin, she started searching the house. Adrenaline took over; she was shaking and terrified again. She didn't know the layout and she couldn't see anything, anyway. She went into a large room dominated by a large, empty crate. There was a doorway at the other end, and she approached it. It took her a moment to work up sufficient courage to open it.

She opened the door, to find bricks and mortar from threshold to transom.

This was done to keep me trapped inside with Kralik, to make sure I couldn't escape. Either I would have to kill him, or he would kill me.

Those butchers. Those incredible butchers.

Suddenly the front door slammed shut.

I'm not alone in this maze, she realized. She began to freak out, and she wasn't sure she was going to be able to stop.

Oh, my God, she thought. *Oh, my God, oh, my God . . .*

After Buffy fled, Giles remained at the library, retreating to the relative comfort of his office. He was deeply distressed, yet fiercely glad he had told her the truth. Now his phone was to his ear, determined to end this wretched situation once and for all. But no one was picking up the phone at the boardinghouse. As he listened to the incessant ringing, Giles figured that for a very bad sign. With each second, his anxiety skyrocketed.

As did his wrath.

Then Quentin Travers walked into the library, and Giles hung up.

"I was trying to reach you," he told the senior Council member.

"I was on watch, by the boardinghouse," Quentin informed him.

"Then you know what's happened." Giles's tone was crisp, angry.

"Yes." Quentin was somber, but he didn't sound—or appear—particularly contrite.

"He's killed Hobson. And made Blair one of his own," Giles continued, in case Quentin didn't realize the enormity of the situation. But the other man remained impassive. Giles flared with anger. "Your perfectly controlled test has spun rather impressively out of control, don't you think?"

Quentin didn't grace his outburst with a reply.

"Well, then, allow me." Giles raised his chin slightly. "I've told Buffy everything."

The older man finally showed some emotion. "That is in direct opposition to the Council's orders."

"Yes. Interestingly enough, I don't give a rat's ass about the Council's orders," Giles snapped. "There will be no test."

"The test has already begun," Quentin countered, with a hint of victory. Giles stared at him, and the man added, "Your slayer entered the field of play about ten minutes ago."

Giles was stunned. "Why . . . ?"

"I don't know. I returned there just as she entered." *That creature's after her. It will kill her.*

Without another moment's thought, Giles started for the door. Moving quickly, Quentin blocked his way, looking stern and reproving. "Giles," he said, "we have no business—"

"This isn't business," Giles bit off.

He would have decked Quentin Travers—*hell, I'd*

kill him—if the Council's man had tried to stop him from going to Buffy's side.

I'll kill anyone—anything—that so much as touches her. . . .

Buffy smelled blood, and death, and danger. She heard nothing.

She both did, and didn't, want to find her mother here.

Her shoes sifting through debris and objects that gave way beneath her weight, she took the measure of the disgusting maze-like prison the Council had created for her. *My birthday present,* she thought angrily. *Congratulations on your years of service, Slayer Summers . . . oh, and as a thank you for all your hard work and surviving this long, we'll try to kill you on your big day.*

Back in the parlor of the Sunnydale Arms, Buffy didn't want to let go of her weapons bag, but she couldn't heft it around any longer. She put it down, hyperalert for any telltale clanking of metal on metal, and inched forward, crossbow at the ready. She went back to the front door. It was shut tight, and she couldn't get it back open.

She began to turn, and that was when the vampire leaped out behind her. She spun and fired, but as with her library target practice, her aim was off. The bolt went wild, and the vampire—not Kralik, but his minion—grabbed the crossbow and wrenched it away from her. Then he grabbed her throat, cutting off her air supply. It hurt, but she didn't give up, even though she began to weaken from lack of oxygen. Spots danced against the pitch darkness. Her legs were on fire.

At last she wriggled free, though she had no idea how she managed it. Running for her life, she ducked into the next room, racing for her weapons bag behind the sofa. The vamp was right behind her, and the sofa was just another brief deterrent in his relentless pursuit of her; he climbed onto it, grabbing at her over the back of it. She scuttled away, no time to get a weapon, panting and gasping. Her lungs were blazing. She was cut and bruised and so afraid, she saw spots in front of her eyes.

He came around the sofa, and Buffy backed up next to a bookcase. Still he came, and she pulled the bookcase down on him. Lots of heavy things fell on him; they would have squashed a human being. Only his head and an arm were exposed. Dazed, he grabbed Buffy's ankle, and she grabbed a table lamp. She slammed it down on his head over and over and over again, until his hand went limp.

Buffy couldn't catch her breath. Beyond freaked; she was really beginning to lose it. But she made herself grab her bag, taking the whole thing with her.

No way am I going to be unarmed in this chamber of horrors.

She was back in the hall of the not-fun house, moving slowly out, looking around. She had no idea where to go; she thought about the stairs, then about continuing down the hall. She moved that way experimentally, when a chilling whisper washed over her in Surround-Sense:

"Hide and seek!"

Oh, God. Does he know where I am?

She swallowed hard and strained to pinpoint the whereabouts of the whisperer. It took an act of will to keep her teeth from chattering. She listened for footfalls, the creaking of the floor, anything to reveal the enemy.

The second time, it was louder. "Hide and seek!"

She spun, still unable to detect the source, barely able to keep from dissolving into sheer panic. It was nearly impossible to hear anything over the pounding of her heart. Blood roared in her ears, and she knew she had to stay calm, knew she had to keep focused or she would fail her mother, and they would both die.

There was the crate again, closed. *Did they keep Kralik inside it? Did it help keep him insane, so he'd do his best to kill me?*

As she regarded it, approaching, Kralik leaped out like a demonic jack-in-the-box, and grabbed her.

Buffy squirmed, fighting his grasp for all she was worth.

Kralik only smiled.

"Why did you come to the dark of the wood . . . ," he said in an obscenely intimate voice, taking her weapons bag with one hand, looking into it, "to bring all these sweets to Grandmother's house?"

He tossed the bag aside and grabbed her with his other hand. His fangs glistened in the half-light, as if he were a slavering beast.

Which he is . . . Buffy thought, unwillingly breathing in his reeking breath. He smelled like rotten meat and his hands were ice cold. *Oh, Mom, I'm so, so sorry . . .*

Then she remembered the cross in the pocket of her overalls, and pulled it out. She brandished it, holding it toward him, and he let go of her at once, hissing.

Weapons, she thought, moving toward the bag. *Whatever I can get my hands on, I'll take him out with it. Even if I have to carve him into pieces with a Swiss Army knife. . . .*

Then he surprised her again, grabbing her hand with the cross still in it. He pulled open his jumpsuit and shoved the cross against his flesh. His chest began to smoke, and he grinned lasciviously.

Then he moved her hand down just a bit to his stomach, and murmured, "A little lower. There," as if she were scratching an itch for him.

Then he moved it lower still, beaming, leering, savoring her humiliation.

Buffy jerked her hand away, frightened and repulsed.

She bolted away from him, racing down the hall without a second look back and throwing herself into the kitchen.

She slammed the door behind her, aware that it was very old and half-rotted, then scanned around for something, anything, she could use as a weapon. There was nothing, and if she cowered there behind the flimsy door, she'd be reduced to nothing as well. Her only hope was to keep moving, keep searching for a means to defeat the enemy. If fighting was out, she'd have to find another way. She was all she had.

I've got to be enough, just me. I've got to be.

She fled through the other side of the kitchen, back into the hall, at the opposite end from the front door, under the stairs.

The stairs. Mom.

Anxiously, she moved slowly toward the foot of the staircase. She was so tense she was afraid one of her muscles would snap—or rather, all of them, along with her nerves—as she waited for Kralik to leap out at her. But he didn't show, and she took the chance to climb as fast as she could.

But he was faster. His hand burst through the rails and grabbed her ankle. One yank and she tumbled back down, hitting her head slamming hard against a step. A white flash of pain signaled a blackout, but she came to in the next second. He was still grabbing at her, snarling, but retreating—*yes, please, yes*—as she fumbled for a splintered rail and jabbed it at his face. He snarled and withdrew, giving her the space to get up.

Blood streamed down her face. *Head wounds are real bleeders for normal people,* she reminded herself. As the Slayer, she was accustomed to the luxury of accelerated healing powers. Hand to her head to staunch the flow, she limped up the stairs as Kralik came around to the foot of the staircase.

Then she was in the upstairs hallway, and she crossed

the first transom she saw. Once inside her momentary refuge, she slammed and bolted the door, knowing full well even as she did so that she was buying only seconds, if that.

The room was pitch-back, and she had no idea if anything else lurked within, if she had been herded inside so something else could do Kralik's dirty work for him. It smelled ugly in there, sour and dirty, and Buffy's skin crawled as stumbled, looking for a light. Her head was bleeding more profusely, and her forehead was on fire.

As she had expected, Kralik slammed with his full weight against the other side door. He was obviously trying to break through, and she knew he'd eventually manage it. He struck it again, using his hard-to-hurt vampire body like a battering ram, and Buffy figured it would take as few as two or three more attempts before the barrier gave way.

Then what?

Now what?

Fear combined with loss of blood were taking their inevitable toll; she was having trouble thinking coherently, and she knew if she stood rooted to the same spot, mired in confusion, she would be dead in less than a minute.

But I don't . . . I don't know what to do . . . I'm dizzy. I'm scared.

As the vampire threw himself against the door again, Buffy swayed in the darkness.

How could this happen? How could Giles sacrifice me like this?

Then her hand brushed a dangling light cord. Instantly she pulled it.

The harsh light of the suspended bare bulb illuminated the room. Dirty, sallow light revealed hundreds and hundreds of Polaroids taped to the walls. Sickened, she saw that each one was of her mother, bound, gagged, terrified. Every square inch of the walls was decorated with them.

Mom, oh, my God, Mom . . .

She completely lost it, and then she forced down her fear once more and took a closer look at one of the photos.

Mom, I'm so sorry. You look so . . .

Buffy blinked at the object behind her mother in the picture.

It's a boiler. She's in the basement.

Kralik's fist burst through the door and flailed for the bolt to get in. There was another door on the other side of the room; Buffy took the escape route and ran back into the hall, most definitely the rat in the maze . . . pursued by a velociraptor.

To one side was a laundry chute. The other led back downstairs, and Buffy headed that way.

The monster stepped into her path, grabbing her again. His fun-and-games smile had disappeared.

"If you stray from the path, you will lose your way," he told her.

Then he bore down on her neck; she fought wildly but *I'm just a girl, just a girl, not the Slayer anymore, oh, God, he's going to bite me.*

As he positioned his mouth over her, he whispered urgently, "I won't take it all. I won't take it all."

Then I'll change, she realized. *I'll be like him. He wants me to be like him. No. Oh, please, no . . .*

Then he reared back roaring, and clutching his head. He was in terrible agony; she didn't understand, it but she didn't plan to stick around and find out what was going on.

As she tried to get by him, he slammed her against the wall. Dazed, she watched as he fumbled in the pocket of his jumpsuit and pulled out a bottle of pills. He was in such pain that his hands were shaking, making it difficult to open the bottle.

Weapon, Buffy thought instinctually. She darted forward and grabbed the bottle. His fury was immediate, uncontrollable; and she raced away with the bottle grasped like a life ring, flinging herself into the laundry chute.

He barreled after her as she shot down, briefly thinking of the vampire in the playground and how easily she had flung him down the slide . . . only to nearly die at his hands a few moments later.

I was stronger then. And that vamp was weaker than Kralik. If Kralik reaches me . . .

I can't let that happen.

I won't let it happen.

Mercifully, Kralik was too big to fit through the chute. He was screaming with frustration, rage, and pain. Buffy slammed down onto the ground so hard, she almost couldn't get up, but she knew she couldn't relax her pace. As frantic as he was, he would still come for his pills. She probably had less than seconds to get the hell out of there.

Then she heard her mother's voice, very muffled.

"Buffy?"

Buffy looked up. Her mother was tied to a chair, and she was bruised and bloodied. Her eyes were huge, but the flesh around them was swollen.

He hurt my mother.

In that moment, Buffy felt the tide turn. All her fear transformed into a rage surpassing Kralik's.

Nobody hurts my mother. Nobody.

Buffy was bloodied, trembling . . . and ready to take on an army of vampires, if they came after Joyce Summers.

"Buffy, we have to get—"

Buffy put her fingers to her lips. She looked around

for a weapon, and a thought began to crystallize. . . .

Then the basement door was blown off its hinges by the force of Kralik's blow. He half-threw himself down the stairs, shrieking, "Where are they? *Where are they?*"

He was dazed with pain; therefore, twice as lethal. He crashed into the cellar, talking quick stock. He looked slightly relieved upon seeing Joyce still tied up.

Buffy tried to slip by him, but he grabbed her, throwing her hard against the wall. He pulled the pills from her fingers and ripped off the top, pouring them into his mouth. His water glass was on a stool, full, and he washed his medication down.

Yes, Buffy thought.

His pain subsided almost immediately. She could see the relief on his face. Then he turned to Buffy, who stood watching expectantly, hopefully.

I can't be wrong about this. It has to work.

"You don't seem to understand your place in all of this," he said. "Do you have any idea—"

Then he stopped, sudden pain wrenching his gut. He was still holding the glass and the bottle of pills as he stared uncomprehendingly at Buffy.

"Oh, my," he breathed. "What did you . . . my pills . . ."

Very calmly, Buffy held up a small, and now empty, container.

Of holy water.

Kralik's eyes went wide. They bulged as he looked down at his body. His stomach smoked and sizzled, eaten away from the inside. Then his entire frame began to tremble and crack.

Savoring his imminent defeat, Buffy said to him, "If I was at full Slayer power, I'd be punning right about now."

Then Kralik exploded. It was beyond a dusting. It was total annihilation.

Buffy stared her deadpan warrior stare at the space where he used to be. *Maybe later, I'll feel more than deadly hatred,* she thought. *For Kralik, for the Council, for Giles . . . Maybe I'll feel like a teenager again, tell Xander the story, and watch him do his victory dance.*

Or not. Maybe this is what growing up is all about for the Slayer.

A moment later, she dropped to Joyce's side and tried to untie her.

"Buffy, thank God you're okay," her mom said as her gag was removed. "Oh, that man . . ."

"I can't get these," Buffy confessed, frustrated. "They're too tight."

"Can't you just—?"

"Not right now," Buffy said, saving the explanation for later. "Maybe there's some clippers."

She moved away . . . and the other vampire, the one she'd knocked out underneath the bookcase, shadowed her, looking pissed.

"Buffy!" Joyce cried.

As Buffy spun, the vampire made his attack—and was tackled from the side by none other than Giles.

Watcher and vampire flew like projectiles, crashing into a tool shelf. The vampire got his footing first and turned on Giles, punching him with jaw-snapping force.

Rushing to Giles's aid, Buffy looked around for a weapon. Before she could locate one, a stake popped out of the vampire's back. Giles had done the deed himself.

The vampire dusted. Buffy figured he had just joined Zackary Kralik in hell, where they belonged.

Buffy stared at Giles, and he back at her. She couldn't read his expression, and she had no idea if he could tell what she was thinking. She couldn't tell, either. She wasn't sure where Giles belonged, as far as she was concerned. . . .

* * *

There was far more hostility in Buffy's stare as Quentin Travers of the Watchers Council of Britain said to her, "Congratulations. You pass."

They were in the library—she and Giles and the idiot from England. Buffy sat at the table, a wet cloth against the deep gash on her forehead. Nobody looked like the hills were alive.

"You exhibited extraordinary courage and clearheadedness in battle. The Council is very pleased."

She glared at him. "Do I get a gold star?"

He was barely perturbed. "I understand that you're upset—"

"You understand nothing," she snapped at him. "You set that monster loose and he came after my *mother*."

"You think the test was unfair?"

Buffy was rendered speechless by the man's unbelievable callousness. Finally she said, in a very dangerous tone, "I think you'd better leave town before I get my strength back."

And still he persisted, either unaware or disinterested in how he was being received. "We're not in the business of 'fair,' Miss Summers. We're fighting a war."

Giles spoke up then. "You're *waging* a war. She's fighting it. There is a difference."

Quentin looked mildly put out. "Mr. Giles, if you don't mind—"

"The test is done. We're finished," Giles said firmly.

"Not quite," Quentin cut in. "She passed. You didn't."

Giles fell silent, and Buffy had no idea what to say.

Quentin continued: "The Slayer isn't the only one who must perform in this situation. I have recommended to the Council, and they have agreed, that you be relieved of your duties as Watcher effectively immediately. You're fired."

Giles finally said, "On what grounds?"

"Your affection for your charge has rendered you incapable of clear and impartial judgment. You have a father's love for the child, and that is useless to the cause."

It took Buffy to absorb the truth of it. *He cares about me. He loves me.*

Giles would not look at her. It was his British way.

"It would be best if you had no further contact with the Slayer," the older Council member added.

"I'm not going anywhere," Giles announced.

"No, well, I didn't expect you to adhere to that. However, if you interfere with the new Watcher or countermand his authority in any way, you'll be dealt with. Are we clear?"

And Rupert Giles, who had once been dubbed "Ripper," gave Quentin Travers a deadly expression and said, "We're very clear."

Quentin said to Buffy, "Congratulations again."

Buffy raised her chin. "Bite me."

"Yes. Well." Quentin threw a look at Giles, and walked out.

Silence took the place of words as Watcher and Slayer stayed where they were, a tableau of unspoken rushes of words. Buffy put the washcloth to the gash on her head and winced.

Giles moved to her, instinctively, tenderly. She looked up at him; there was more silence, and then she handed him the rag.

That single gesture said so much, and he found himself remembering the words of a poem he had written upon finally accepting his Calling as a Watcher, a defeat he had fought so long and so hard to avoid. The tattered piece of paper lay pressed between the pages of his journal, and from time to time he unfolded it and read it, though he had long ago committed the words to memory:

> *I shall never be forgiven all my faults, by man*
> *nor god nor*
> *any*
> *good*
> *thing.*

> *But this I know: I am not here for grace,*
> *nor pardon,*
> *nor to give them.*

> *My way is through shadow,*
> *blackness on the path, and in my*
> *heart,*
> *in my eyes,*
> *and in my soul.*

> *My fate . . .*
> *unknown.*
> *My destiny . . .*
> *my own.*

Acutely aware of his shortcomings as a man and as a Watcher . . . *and as a poet* . . . he tended lovingly—paternally—to Buffy, and she allowed it.

Words will not express this moment, he thought to himself, *but I'll put something in my journal about it . . . even though I'm no longer a Watcher and therefore, have no obligation to do so.*

I do, however, have a need to. All my life, I've kept a journal, knowing someday other eyes would read my words. I shall do it for Buffy. I owe her so much more than that.

* * *

Much with the peanut buttery goodness in Buffy's kitchen, as once more, she had triumphed over the evil that was her birthday. Her friends were slathering Jiff all over thick bread, and her mom was bustling in that happy mom way when one knows where one's kid is and all her fellow ones are safely captive in Mom Central—aka, the kitchen.

Willow said, not for the first time, "I can't believe Giles was fired! How could Giles be fired?"

Oz opted for a change of tune. "So how did you manage to kill Kralik?"

"Oh, she was very clever," Joyce said brightly, then caught Buffy's *hey, that's my story* look and added, "You go ahead and tell it, dear. You tell it better."

Willow was not to be deterred. "Now, when you say fired, you mean *fired?*"

Xander performed the nonverbal equivalent of clearing his throat by sliding a glance at his childhood chum. "You're not cruising past that concept any time soon, are you?"

She wasn't. "It's just, I mean, he's been *fired!* He's unemployed! He's between jobs!"

They needed more peanut butter, and Joyce, with her mom radar, bustled off to get some out of the pantry. Bustle, bustle, bustle.

So why did they call those big padded butt-things "bustles" back in the olden days? Buffy wondered, as she said to her very favorite, very concerned redheaded best friend, "Giles isn't going anywhere, Will. He's still librarian."

Willow made her grumpy face. "Okay, but I'm writing an angry letter."

Buffy was amused. Willow's mom was big with the letter-writing to protest against injustice. She must have passed her social-activist gene on to her daughter.

"Nothing's really gonna change. The important thing is, I kept up my special birthday tradition of gut-wrenching misery and horror."

Oz gave her a nod. "Bright side to everything."

The fresh peanut butter having materialized, thanks to the transporter machine that was her mother, Buffy grabbed it and tried to open the jar. It was not cooperative, and she frowned mildly at it. "I'll just feel better when I get my strength back." She tried again, failed again.

Xander smiled at her with a superior air of condescension. "Give you a hand with that, little lady?"

Buffy gave him playful eye-daggers along with the jar. "You're loving this far too much," she drawled.

He took the jar and grinned at her. "Admit it. Sometimes you just need a big—" he starting twisting— "strong" —kept twisting, but nothing happened— "man. . . ."

He struggling manfully on, smiling most manfully, fully unable to manhandle the peanut butter into submission.

Finally, he murmured sheepishly (but in a manfully sheepishly manner), "Uh, Will? Give me a hand with that?"

You were her father, and you betrayed her, Krathalal said.

Giles looked up from his journal, which he realized he had been reading aloud to the demon, and stared into the waves of flame before and around him, the heat blistering his flesh. From his otherworldly perspective, he saw that the green fires from his magick circle had separated and re-formed into three concentric circles, and that he had crossed through the first circle. The one he faced now raged more violently than the previous, and the third was a veritable firestorm in which he could not hope to survive.

He told the demon, "We dealt with that."

But it signaled a rift. She never fully trusted you again. Never turned to you to make things right as eagerly.

Giles sincerely doubted that. To the demon god, he said, "Why are you asking me about these things? How will they help you protect Buffy?"

They won't.

Giles pressed the book against his chest. "Then why—"

"Why ask you to read from your journal, as if I want a bedtime story? I want your sacrifice to mean something, Krathalal informed him, in sounds of crackling wood and skin and the acrid stench of burning human hair. *I crave from you . . . informed consent.*

"You have it," Giles insisted. "Now. I give it to you freely."

Prove it.

We will speak of her next birthday, after she had left the Council. She was in college then, and you were not her Watcher. You had no job, no calling, no reason for being. Your heart was broken.

Giles frowned. "That's ridiculous. Perhaps I had a small midlife crisis, but—"

Step into the second circle of fire. And we will see.

Giles obeyed.

It was excruciating. The heat curled around his heart, and the blood inside it began to curdle, like milk. Red steam rose from his pores, and as he looked, huge pieces of skin from his arms sizzled like strips of bacon. It put him in mind of how a Ethurian Fire Serpent shed its skin.

Read from your book. She was in college, then . . .

"I don't think this will be useful," he protested.

Read.

Or no deal.

Speak the words of your shame and inadequacy.

"Oh, very well," Giles grumbled, capitulating.

With fingers that had become little more than charred bones, he opened his journal to the section about Buffy's nineteenth birthday, and read to the creature.

"A New Man"

The moon had yet to rise, and the dorm room was dark save for the bedside lamp that threw a romantic glow over the two bodies lying on Buffy's bed in the UC Sunnydale dorm room she shared with Willow.

Well, usually with Willow. Right now, I'm sharing it with Riley.

On the eve of her nineteenth birthday, all was very good with the world. She and the gang had defeated the Mayor, graduated from Sunnydale High, which was now a pile of rubble, and she had made it to *ta-dah!* college. Just like other girls, she was taking freshman classes, and when she wasn't dusting Big Vamps on Campus like Sunday or getting involved with the wrongest kind of guys, she was doing a pretty good job of growing up.

And Happy Birthday, Buffy . . . she and her former psych TA were kissing.

It's like good cocoa, Buffy thought, both hot and sweet. *Smoochies with Riley Finn, my tall, nice human guy*

with honey-colored hair and sweet eyes that make me rip-
ple and a wicked-cocoa smile, and chocolate kisses . . .

Riley murmured, "We're not expecting anyone, are
we?"

She smiled at him, knowing what he was really asking her, and shook her head. "Willow said she was going
to be at the science library all night."

"Is that right?" Riley's voice was husky. He held her,
pulling Buffy down to him, and they kissed again, hard.
He smelled of soap and shampoo, and many other good
things. His eyes were clear and sparkly, and there were
dimples at the corners of his mouth. He wasn't a user like
stinky Parker man, and he wasn't dead and broody, like
Angel.

No one's like Angel, she thought, then, feeling dis-
loyal, reminded herself, *Riley is the one I really want.*
And amazingly enough, he's okay to want. 'Course, we
had that rough patch when I found out he was a super-
secret soldier in the Initiative, and he was upset 'cause I
didn't tell him about my slayage gig, but all in all, we're
dealing. He's not gonna send the world to hell or hurt my
feelings . . . at least I don't think . . . or vamp out or any-
thing if I . . . if we . . .

Oh, yay . . .

He started to pull her shirt up, and Buffy warmed all
over, eager, a little shy, but good with it, excellent with
it—and that was when Willow burst in, out of breath.

"Apparently not," Buffy murmured.

As Buffy smoothed her clothing, they both looked
questioningly at the redheaded witch, who blurted,
"We've got trouble!"

Buffy sighed. "What's up?" she asked, already feeling herself slipping into the mindset of the Slayer. There
would be no more hot chocolate tonight.

Willow barely took in the evidence of their recent

and big-time *der smoochens.* "I was in the rec room," she said, sucking in air. "It came in through the window."

"Vampire?" Riley asked, all business.

Willow shook her red hair. "Vampires don't breathe fire."

Buffy grabbed her weapons bag, and she and Riley followed Willow out of their dorm room and into the hall, which was strangely quiet. Stevenson Hall was not famed for its partying the way Porter Hall was, but it wasn't a monastery, either. When they reached the rec room doors, Buffy pulled out a crossbow and handed it to Riley as he said quietly, "I should call for backup."

"No time," she replied, gesturing toward the door father away from them. Riley started toward it as Buffy turned to the nearer door, reaching for the knob. As her hand closed on it, she whispered to Willow, "I wanna make this fast. I really had better things to do tonight than kill." Not that she and Riley were likely to recapture the moment, but one never knew . . .

She flung the door open, her hand clasped on an ax inside her weapons bag.

In a burst of blinding brilliance, all the lights came on. Giles, Xander, and Anya—not to mention a couple dozen dormies, most of whom Buffy recognized—leaped out from behind any and all possible hiding places—couches, tables, pinball machines . . .

Buffy froze in her tracks, hand reflexively gripping the ax haft, pulling it partially free of the bag before she realized what was going on.

"Surprise!" everyone chorused.

Buffy lowered the bag to the floor. From the corner of her eye she noticed Riley entering through the other door, apparently equally thrown off guard. He stashed the crossbow behind a chair.

It's a birthday party, Buffy realized. *They've thrown me a surprise birthday party.*

Willow looked at the speechless birthday girl and grinned. "Guess you won't be killing anything tonight after all," she said, chortling.

The Slayer smiled, a scary forced rictus lighting up her face. "Don't be so sure," she murmured through clenched teeth. . . .

Okay, it was fun. She had to admit that; therefore, she was less inclined to slaughter her dear, good-hearted friends, who had gone to a lot of work to make sure she did not celebrate her birthday privately, with Agent Finn. Music played, and people ate and talked. And ate. *Xander must have had something to do with the munchies,* she thought. There were potato chips, pretzels, Snickers bars, and lots of other faboo junk.

There was also a huge birthday cake with a Supergirl figurine on it, a nice in-joke, which she and Willow were in the process of cutting. It felt surprisingly normal to be slicing food with a kitchen knife, even though the last time she had held one, she had used it to cut the throat of a Green Mountain demon.

Giles, Xander, and Anya stood to one side, observing the frolicking. "This is rather like an activities room we had back at public school," Giles reminisced. "One time I got up to a bit of a prank with the dartboard—"

"I'm bored," Anya interrupted, speaking to Xander. "Let's eat."

Xander looked exasperated, in a patient, long-suffering kind of way. "Anya, we talked about this."

The former vengeance demon rolled her eyes, then turned to Giles and said as if by rote, "I'm sorry. That was rude. Please continue with your story. I hope it involves treacle and a headmaster."

"Go eat," Giles said, also in a patient, long-suffering kind of way.

Anya happily grabbed Xander and pulled him toward the food. Xander shot an apologetic smile back at the Watcher as they disappeared into the crowd.

Giles moved back into the shadow of a bookcase, once again letting British reserve dictate his actions and feelings. As always, he felt most comfortable observing people from a distance, as opposed to mingling with them.

A Watcher, indeed, he thought. *What an appropriate job title.*

He had planned to celebrate Buffy's birthday alone, working on his journal as he toasted his girl's achievement of surviving to the ripe old age of nineteen. Many previous Slayers had not, and it behooved him to write about her remarkable life. In so many ways, Buffy did not fit the Slayer mold as defined by the Watchers Council of Britain. For one thing, she had died, then was brought back with CPR. For another, she had fought alongside her successor, Kendra, called by her brief death, and survived the poor girl.

Then there was the matter of Faith, Kendra's successor, who had tried to kill both Buffy and Angel. She now lay in a coma. Buffy had left the Council and was a maverick Slayer, but Faith had been a rogue Slayer, one of the most dangerous beings on the planet.

Giles, too, was no longer of the Council, and with the Sunnydale High School library a pile of ash, he was also unemployed. He continued to fight the good fight as best he could, offering advice to the Slayer upon occasion, but her birthday served to remind him that she was growing up.

Willow stepped up behind him, startling him from his reverie. Willow had matured from a gangly, shy social outcast to a Wicca of no small power. She'd survived her childhood infatuation for Xander and endured the loss of Oz. He sincerely hoped she found a new romance that was kinder to her than her previous ones had proven to be.

"Hey, Giles. Having a good time?"

Of a sort, he thought mildly. "Yes," he fibbed. "There are a lot of new faces here, aren't there?"

"Uh-huh. Mostly kids from the dorm. And a couple of Riley's friends."

Riley, Giles echoed to himself. He didn't know who that was. He supposed it wasn't particularly important. As Buffy and her friends expanded their social circles, he didn't expect to be kept abreast of their new friendships. Indeed, it had been rather wearying, listening to the details of high school existence: who was wearing what, who was dating whom, which teachers were "mean," and how all of them wanted to be done with school, once and for all . . . so that they could attend college.

At that moment, Buffy joined them, with a tall, nice-looking young man in tow. "Hey, Giles," she said.

She looked lovely, a young lady indeed, so poised and so very capable. Giles surprised both her and himself by giving her a nice, warm hug. "Buffy, Happy Birthday," he said to her. "Nineteen. Hard to believe, isn't it? I—"

Buffy interrupted in a burst of teenage impatience. "Giles, I want you to meet someone." She pulled the lad forward. "This is Riley Finn. My boyfriend." She glanced at this Riley, as if to check to see how he was handling the situation. He was beaming, and she was beaming back.

Ah. This is Riley, he who has brought his friends, he thought, with a little tug at his fatherly heart. *He is Buffy's new love.*

Riley shook Giles's hand. "Very nice to meet you, Mr. Giles. Did you help plan this? It was quite a surprise."

A young American who shakes hands and calls me "Mr. Giles." How refreshing. And yet, she could have mentioned him before now. . . .

To give himself a moment, Giles polished his glasses. "First of many," he replied. "You've been . . . dating long?"

Someone tapped Willow's arm and pulled her into a neighboring conversation as Buffy explained to Riley, "Giles was the librarian at my school."

"I've seen the library," Riley told Giles. "It's gone downhill since you left."

Giles chuckled, surprised at how easily the mirth came. *He's a nice lad. Quick-witted.* "Yes, I'm embarrassed to say I actually miss it at times."

"So, you're retired?" Riley asked.

"I'm sorry?" Giles was aghast. *Good heavens. I'm only . . . not old enough to retire. Perhaps if I were a cricket player, or a mountain climber. But a sedentary librarian?*

Good Lord.

"Or you're working somewhere else now?" Riley said quickly, a deft save if Giles had ever profited before by one.

"Well, not . . . I'm sort of between projects just now," Giles prevaricated. *Does that signify that I actually am retired? What a thoroughly depressing thought.*

"Riley! Oh!" Buffy grabbed him and pointed in the direction of the birthday goodies. "Look at this. Giles has no cake!"

"Oh, hey." Riley looked vastly relieved, as if he knew he had committed a faux pas and needed a tactful way to extricate his foot from his mouth. "I'll get you a piece." He peeled off to do just that.

Buffy smiled at Giles. "He's a little nervous." She hesitated, then continued. "You know, it's nice having everyone together for my birthday. Of course, you could smash all my toes with a hammer and it would still be the bestest Buffy birthday in a good long while."

Giles was mortified as he recalled the events of last year. "Right. Well, Xander and Willow did all the planning. Not sure I'd have gone with a surprise party. You've enough things jumping out at you in the dark. Don't know if you need the extra adrenaline."

"Professor Walsh says adrenaline is like exercise but without the exorbitant gym fees," Buffy informed him.

"Very witty." Though he may not have heard about Riley before, he had heard about Professor Walsh. In fact, Professor Walsh was one of the enduring subjects of Buffy's conversation these days. He was certain that at this point he had enough data on her to write her biography.

Buffy nodded. "You should meet Professor Walsh. She's absolutely the smartest person I ever met."

Giles could not help sounding a trifle peevish as he said, "Perhaps we should have invited Professor Walsh to the party."

Buffy shook her head. "Oh, no. She's, like, forty. The last thing she'd want to do is hang out with a bunch of kids."

Unlike myself, she means. As for being, like, forty—

Further conversation was interrupted by Riley's return. He had a piece of cake on a plate, which he handed to Giles. "Here you go, sir."

Giles accepted it and dutifully put a forkful in his mouth. After all, it was Buffy's birthday cake. And for American preprocessed baked goods, it wasn't bad.

And I certainly have nothing better to do. . .

The next day, at *Casa del Xand*, Spike was moving out—a happy occurrence that couldn't happen soon enough for Mister Landlord. Spike had hardly been the best of houseguests, despite the fact that Riley's secret little Army Corps of Bioengineers, aka the Initiative, had defanged Spike by putting a chip in his head. It rendered him totally unable to hurt human beings with so much as a gentle slap, much less bite them in standard-issue fang manner.

But that didn't turn Spike into a nice guy. Oh, no. It didn't mean he picked up after himself or said "please" and "thank you." If anything, it made the white-haired vampire more surly and unsociable than he had been in the first place.

Which, score one for the Army guys—making Spike even less civilized is quite an accomplishment.

Xander watched, along with Anya, as the vampire stuffed drip bags full of blood and a carton of cigarettes, among other things, into a duffel bag. Xander could barely keep from doing the Snoopy dance as he fanned away the acrid fumes of Spike's stinky cig with one hand. No more refrigerator filled with canisters of blood and plasma, looking like it came from an ER. No more basement filled with secondhand smoke from the vampire's filthy habit.

In short, no more Spike.

He couldn't wait. Impatiently, he said, "You own nothing. This shouldn't be taking so long."

"Hang on," Spike replied. "Let a fellow get organized."

He put a portable radio in his bag. Xander recognized and protested, "That's my radio!"

Spike glowered at him. "And you're what, shocked and disappointed? I'm evil!"

No, Xander thought. *The Borgias were evil. You barely qualify as petty.* But he kept his mouth shut. Conversation would only delay Spike's imminent departure.

Anya sought as well to defer more bickering. "So,"

she said, paging through a magazine, "what kind of a place are you looking for?"

The vampire shrugged. "Dunno," he admitted. "Maybe a crypt. Or a sewer. Someplace that's, you know, dark and dank." He glanced around the basement in distaste. "But not as dark and dank as this."

"It's pretty depressing, isn't it?" Anya tossed off.

Hey, Xander thought, but he didn't say anything. All the other Scoobs were off in college, making something of themselves, and blue-collar guy had been left behind to make nickels and dimes via dead-end jobs. So far, Anya had stuck with him. But for how much longer?

"I've known corpses with a fresher spell. Matter-of-fact, I've been one." Spike tapped ash onto the floor.

Seething, Xander pointed to the ashtray sitting right next to the vamp. In response, Spike flicked the butt at Xander. The latter jerked a thumb at the stairs.

"That's it. Let's go."

Spike looked at Xander, apparently realizing at last that if he didn't leave now he'd be sleeping in an urn on the mantelpiece. He picked up his bag and started to go.

Anya said, "Wait. I want to give you something for your new place."

Xander silently groaned. He misquoted Henry the Somethingth of England to himself— *"Will no one rid me of this worrisome undeadbeat?"* Whoever he had been, that king had had the good sense to murder his archbishop so that it could be made into a film that, frankly, had not stood the test of time, but which allowed Xander, King of Mildew, to catch up on his sleep while it was shown in World Civilization back in far happier times known as the days of high school.

Seized with inspiration, Anya picked up a lamp and handed it to Spike.

"That's my *lamp!*" Xander protested, staring at Anya in disbelief.

She returned the look blandly. "A gift is traditional. I read about it."

"That's among *friends,*" Xander explained. "With bitter enemies, we don't give them my lamp."

"It's not gonna have electricity, anyway," Spike pointed out. "It's a crypt, remember?"

Xander snatched the lamp back from Spike and returned it to its rightful place, on top of the scorch marks his cousin had put there by lighting his far . . . fireworks.

"What about running water?" Anya queried. "A fridge to keep your blood fresh?"

"No," Spike replied, looking mildly concerned.

Anya heaved a sigh. "That's gonna just suck. You should get a hotel room or something."

This was clearly new territory for Spike, who said, "Demon girl's got a point." He looked at Xander. "If I had a few bob for a room with an honor bar . . . "

"Out!" Xander shouted. "Before I get the Slayer over here to kick your ass out."

The vampire frowned, making no move toward the stairs. "Don't know why she didn't come . . . say good-bye, shed a few tears . . ."

Xander retorted, "Well, she has an appointment with someone who's actually still scary."

Spike tossed him a dirty look, but headed up the stairs at last. Anya followed, and Xander brought up the rear.

Never again, he promised himself, *will I open my door to a creature of the night. They're harder to get rid of than my drunken relatives when there's still some Jack Daniel's left in the liquor cabinet.*

With short blonde hair and a good, strong face, Professor Walsh sat at her desk in her office at UC Sunnydale. She was on her turf, in her space, as opposed to Buffy, who sat on the opposite side of her desk, in the uncomfortable place known as the hot seat. Riley stood beside her, all proud guy. Buffy felt like a puppy Riley wanted to keep, and Maggie Walsh had veto power.

"So," Dr. Walsh began. "The Slayer."

Buffy nodded. "Yeah. That's me."

The professor looked pleased. "We thought you were a myth."

Nervously, Buffy gave her a little smile and said, "Well . . . you were myth-taken."

Maggie Walsh stared blankly forward.

Dumb joke, Buffy chided herself.

"And to think, all that time you were sitting in my class. Well, most of those times. I always thought you could have a done better than a B minus." There was a hint of triumph in the professor's voice. "But now I understand that your energies were directed . . . elsewhere."

Buffy tried hard not to look at Riley so she wouldn't give away that, um, "elsewhere" also included lots of places where she and Riley could get to know each other through the time-honored method of making out.

"Our goals are similar," Dr. Walsh continued. "We're each interested in curtailing the subterrestrial menace. It's only our methods that differ." She gestured with her hand. "We use the latest in scientific technology and state-of-the-art weaponry, while you—if I understand this correctly—poke them with a sharp stick."

Buffy tried not to squirm in her seat. "It's more effective than it sounds."

"Oh, I'm quite sure of that." Dr. Walsh grinned, a hint of mischief playing at the corners of her mouth. "And I'm just as sure we can learn much from each other. I'm working on getting you clearance to come into the Initiative. I think you'll find the results of our operation most impressive."

Cool! Buffy thought. *Hey, I'm not in trouble! I'm . . . I'm in!*

The doctor gestured to Riley. "Agent Finn here, alone, has captured or killed . . ." she looked up at him— "how many is it?"

Buffy looked at Riley, too, eager to bask in the glory of being Monster Killer's girlfriend.

Riley straightened slightly, almost as if he were coming to attention. "Seventeen," he said quietly. Buffy could hear the pride in his voice. "Eleven vampires. Six demons."

That's all?! Buffy almost blurted. *Are you kidding? Do you mean seventeen yesterday between classes, or in your whole monster-killing tour of duty?*

Though he wasn't looking at her, Buffy knew that he was hoping for some kind of validation from the Slayer of his kill count. "Huh," she said, trying to inject as much sincerity into her voice as she could. "Well, that is . . . I mean, wow, seventeen." She kept her eyes wide and sincere, suddenly acutely aware that she hadn't read the psych chapter on nonverbal communication all that well . . . and that Professor Walsh was one of the most renowned people in the world on that subject.

Then the professor's attention shifted from her boy wonder to his fluffy puppy, and discomfort speared Buffy like a stake of made of ice. *No,* she thought. *Please don't ask. Please don't.*

"What about you?" Dr. Walsh asked expectantly.

Buffy tried to pretend she didn't understand the question, already knowing resistance was futile. "Me?"

Professor Walsh patiently rephrased the question. "How many hostiles would you say you've . . . slain?"

Oh, crap.

Buffy glanced back at Riley, who was looking straight ahead, then down to her, then back to Walsh. *No way out,* she told herself with a silent sigh. *Lying's only going to make it worse when he does find out that I can basically take seventeen out without chipping a nail.*

So she told them.

It was a perfectly lovely day in Sunnydale, as so many were. People in California liked to brag that they didn't have weather, precisely. They had "climate." Each day was a boring repetition of the next, which was all right, Giles supposed, if all one wanted out of life was a tan.

However, one thing they never talk about in Southern California is the sheer amount of dust that accumulates in a short period, he groused. *It's prodigious.*

Giles was dusting bookshelves in his apartment. It was one of the calming rituals he performed when he was nervous or uncertain. Being a Watcher guaranteed quite a lot of free-floating anxiety at the best of times, but when one was off the job, and yet felt responsible for keeping the forces of evil at bay to at least some extent, anxiety piled up rather like, well, dust.

As the ostrich feathers flicked over the book spines, he stopped. He pulled from the shelf a heavy, iron-hasped volume of ancient lore. He opened it, leafed through the weathered vellum pages, and an obscure reference popped out at him.

The finding caused him to gasp. Slowly, almost unwillingly, he turned his head to look at his desk calendar, then back to the weathered reference. He put the handle of the duster in his mouth, so that he vaguely resembled a flamenco dancer with a rose in her teeth, and carried the book to his couch. There he counted the dates off on his fingers, just to make sure there was no mistake.

There was no mistake.

"Oh, crap," Giles murmured.

* * *

A few moments later, he was picking various thaumaturgic items off his shelves and stuffing them into a small carrying bag. He spoke into his phone and said, "No, we can't wait for her, Willow. The Demon Prince Barvain is going to rise tonight." He listened, then asked, "Well, where *is* she, exactly?"

Her meeting with Dr. Walsh over, Buffy walked with Riley down one of the campus pathways. Their reaction to her kill count had been worse than she'd anticipated—shock, amazement, much with the trading looks—and Buffy really, really wanted to remind Riley that while he had started out as a basic human being and gotten his strength and reflexes the old-fashioned way, she had been born with an extra advantage. Heck, if she tried out for the Olympics and they found out she was a slayer, they'd probably disqualify her. But not him. He'd get to do that one-hundred-meter dash, no questions asked.

But she could feel his gaze on her. He was either freaked out or let down or revved up or all of the above. In anticipation of whichever response he had, Buffy had already opened her mouth a dozen times, only to shut it without saying anything. *What is there to say, really?*

She sneaked a glance at her beau. Riley's face seemed remarkably calm, considering what he'd learned about her. He noticed her looking at him, and essayed something approaching a smile.

"Wow," he said.

Buffy's smile didn't come off all that great, either. Searching for *something* to say that might make him feel better, she said, "But those were my best stories. I didn't tell you the 'Buffy breaks her butt' stories."

They walked on. "But you killed the . . . You did the thing with the . . . and you drowned, and then . . . snake! Not to mention daily slayage of . . . wow."

She shrugged. "No big. Really." Almost desperately, she added, "Hey, who wants ice cream?"

The subject was not closed for Agent Finn, and ice cream was not about to distract him, it appeared. He said, "Buffy, when I saw you stop the world from . . . you know, ending, I just assumed that was a big week for you. Turns out I suddenly find myself . . . needing to know the plural of apocalypses."

I don't cause them, I just avert them, she wanted to remind him. She was so not loving this conversation. *Normal girl, normal guy . . . please, Riley? Just this once, just us? For my birthday present, maybe?*

Drooping, she began to lose hope that he would move on from this topic to something far less exciting. She didn't want Riley to feel intimidated around her. *By* her.

"Look," she ventured, "if you'd been fighting since you were fifteen, you'd have a hefty résumé, too."

Wrong thing to say. Riley's eyes widened in utter disbelief. *"Fifteen—"*

"I know, 'wow,'" she conceded. "But, point is that we have different amounts of experience. Plus, I do have that whole preternatural Slayer strength deal. . . . "

Riley nodded. "I've seen. Don't get me wrong. Girls I grew up with could hold their own, but . . . I'm not even sure *I* could take you."

Buffy gazed up at him. She liked hearing that emphasis on "I." Liked his confidence, his kinda boy-swagger, *only, hey, he's a man; Buffy has graduated to the big leagues, where boyfriends aren't boys and maybe this one has the maturity to realize he isn't less of a guy just because I'm something more than um, human. . . .*

"Well." She gave him a sly grin. "That kind of depends on your meaning."

Mutual smile: a challenge brewing. Riley was good

with a challenge. He was liking a challenge. Liking her. The Slayer.

Yes.

As they walked, they kept talking, and Buffy, slowly, began to get the idea that Riley had a strength of his own. He liked himself. He thought he was a worthwhile person doing a vital service to humanity. He possessed real confidence in his abilities, which were not diminished by his true, sheer enjoyment that she was really, really good at what she did.

This is nice, she thought. *Very nice.*

I could get used to it.

Giles remembered the anxieties of his first days at Oxford, and relived them all as he tried to make his way through the complexities of UC Sunnydale. There were hand-lettered signs informing him of various inconsistencies in the painted signs beside them; places one could park, though not at the moment; offices switched and office hours cancelled or postponed. Directories were incomplete or incorrect.

Students politely passed him, the girls clad in scanty outfits that made him alternately stare and blush. He felt old, out of touch, and out of his element.

Finally Giles stood before an office door, hesitating. He read the plaque of black plastic attached to the door: M. WALSH, PH.D. PSYCHOLOGY. He realized that his hesitation was a combination of uncertainty and nerves, and that he was behaving like a first-form student, not a grown man with pressing business of his own.

Oh, for God's sake, he thought, and rapped sharply on the door.

After a moment, he heard a feminine voice from within say, "Yes?"

Giles opened and entered, resisting the urge to peek

cautiously around it first. "Professor Walsh, I presume," he said warmly to a short-haired, petite woman with pleasing features formed into a quizzical smile. She was much better looking than he'd imagined her to be.

"You're hard to find. These halls are quite the Labyrinth. Felt rather like Theseus." The woman watched him and said nothing. Her gaze was direct, and she looked quite intelligent. "With the Minoutaur," he continued, rambling. "In the . . . labyrinth."

Professor Walsh was not completely cold as she asked, "Can I help you with something, Mr. —?"

"Giles. Rupert." He extended his hand. "I'm looking for Buffy Summers. I'm—I'm a friend of hers."

Professor Walsh looked mildly scandalized, and Giles realized belatedly how his statement might be misinterpreted. "And . . . I was her high school librarian," he added hastily.

This further attempt at clarification did little to soften the woman's expression. He'd rather assumed he might charm her, but that clearly was not about to happen. She was waiting for him to continue, and she was going to do nothing to make him feel comfortable. She simply looked at him expectantly.

Giles wondered what it was about that that was so . . . unmanning. She was not physically imposing by any means, nor was she rude. And yet he suddenly felt that he would rather face a high echelon demonic manifestation than be on her wrong side.

Which you might bloody well find yourself doing, he reminded himself, *if you don't find the Slayer.*

Walsh said, "I'm sorry. Buffy's not here. But if I see her—"

"Buffy has been very influenced by your course," Giles continued. "She quotes you quite often. Sometimes she sounds a bit like an introductory textbook herself."

He realized he was on the verge of babbling, but damn it, the woman seemed to inspire that kind of nervousness.

"I don't lecture from the textbook, but I'm glad she's inspired by the material," Professor Walsh replied. "She's bright. All she's really been lacking is encouragement in the academic setting."

Giles blinked. *I helped her plenty of times,* he silently protested. *We even went over the SAT exams while patrolling in the graveyard.*

"Well, I think it's best if we let a young person find their own strengths," he ventured.

He resisted the urge to remove his glasses and polish them, and it was at that moment he realized that he had first developed the habit at Oxford. Back then, it had been a delaying tactic, a way for him to consider questions without appearing diffident or uncertain of the proper answer. Now, it was simply a bad tic, an automatic response.

"If you lead a child by the hand," he continued, "they never find their own footing. . . ."

Walsh smiled thinly. "And if it's true about hiking, ergo it must be true about life?"

Ooph, how . . . directly rude.

"That's not . . . " Giles realized with a shock that he was perilously close to stuttering. He tried to muster his thoughts, stop rattling on like a prat. "I'm just saying that Buffy isn't the typical student. Once you get to know her, you'll find she's a unique girl. I hope you're not going to push her too—"

"I think I do know her," Walsh said, moving around the room as she put away things or stacked things or whatever it was that professors did when they had assistants and/or papers to grade. "And I have found her to be a unique *woman,*" she continued, putting a subtle but unmistakable emphasis on the last word.

Giles briefly closed his eyes. "Woman. Of course. How wrong of me to choose my own word . . . "

She ignored that, or missed it entirely. "She's very self-reliant, very independent . . ."

Now we're getting somewhere. He warmed to her. "Exactly—"

"Which is not always a good thing," the professor insisted. "It can be unhealthy to take on adult roles too early. What I suspect I'm seeing is a reaction to the absence of a male role model."

Giles felt as if a troll had just kicked him in the gut. "The absence of a . . . ?"

"Buffy clearly lacks a strong father figure."

"I—I," Giles said, knowing full well he was stuttering like an utter weed, and unable to stop. "I—"

Professor Walsh, clearly in control of the conversation now, said, "I'm sorry. I have things to do. I'll tell Buffy her friend was looking for her."

She gave him a "that-is-all" smile. Nonplussed, Giles stood there for another few seconds, then turned and left the office.

He was still feeling the blush of indignation hours later as he led Willow and Xander through the cemetery. It was full dark, the tombstones and mausoleums fitfully illuminated by the moon's leprous light as clouds disinterestedly layered it with gauze. It was a perfect setting to complement Giles's dark broodings on M. Walsh, Ph.D.

He realized Willow was speaking. "This prince demon guy was supposed to rise at sunset. So aren't we, like, late?"

"Yes, well," Giles replied stiffly. "If I hadn't had to search the globe for our Miss Summers and do battle with that harridan . . ."

"And," Xander chimed in, "if you hadn't gotten lost on campus afterward. . . ."

Giles decided not to mention that he'd gotten lost beforehand as well. There was no use handing Xander more ammunition, not when Giles was already feeling shot down. Besides, they were now near the mausoleum where the resurrection was supposed to take place. Giles stopped and drew himself up to his full height.

"Never mind. I'll just have to take care of it myself. Vanquished a few demons without her in my day," he added under his breath. "Of course, it shouldn't take me by surprise if we *are* entirely too late. Demon on the loose, carnage everywhere . . ."

The three continued into one of the larger crypts, which, to their surprise, they found still quiet and neat and, most of all, empty. Added to which there was not the slightest bit of carnage, not even in the dark, hard-to-see corners.

Xander pursed his lips as he looked around. "Your better demons clean up after themselves."

Giles raised the light, looking about in bafflement. "I—I don't understand," he murmured. "There should be ruptured earth, broken stones. . . ."

The Watcher put his weapons bag down in the shadows near the door. As he spoke, he began setting out the ritual items he had packed earlier: a candle, an inscribed stone, a sprig of dried wolfsbane. . . .

"Apparently it hasn't happened yet," he continued. "A bit of luck."

"Or," Willow piped up cheerily, "you know what? I bet the Initiative took care of it."

Giles stopped his preparations and looked at her. "Who?"

"Riley and his guys," Xander explained. "Probably all over it."

Willow nodded in agreement. "It has that 'too neat' look. They must have cleaned up the place."

Giles blinked, uncertain for a moment if he still understood English. "What?"

Willow shifted. "They read hot spots. Areas of other-worldly energy. They must've picked this place up days ago."

Giles raised his hands. "Stop. Both of you." He waited until they were both looking at him expectantly and said, "What's the Initiative, and what does it have to do with Buffy's new boyfriend?"

He realized they were wearing identical expressions of confusion and surprise. They glanced at each other at precisely the same moment, and then Willow said, "You know. I'm sure you know." Her voice became more hesitant as perhaps he *didn't* know. Which he patently did not. "Riley's one of the commandos."

"*What?* Oh, that's marvelous, isn't it," he demanded, throwing up his hands. "Here I've spent weeks trying to get a single scrap of information on our mysterious demon-collectors, and no one bothered to tell me that *Buffy's dating one?*" He stared at the two of them, and they shuffled their feet. "Who else knows this?"

"No one!" Xander promised. "No one knows this." He didn't blink. "Anya. That's it."

They were both silent for a moment. Then Willow said out of the corner of her mouth, "And Spike."

"*Spike?!*" Giles was stunned. "*Spike* knew?"

Xander held out his hands. "Only the basic stuff. Y'know, that Riley's a commando, Professor Walsh is in charge—"

Hello?! He nearly staggered from the blow.

"*Professor Walsh?* That fishwife?"

Willow chewed the inside of her lip. "She's not so bad once you get to—" she must have noticed his glare of loathing and continued seamlessly— "So, the demon's probably a little late. We'll just, you know . . ." She made as if to sit down.

The fight was completely drained out of him. He was a hollow shell. He was a warrior no longer.

"Oh, forget it. You two can leave off. I'll stay a little longer, just in case." He stared down at the things in his hands, feeling the utter fool.

The two young people faced him. Willow said guilelessly, "You sure? 'Cause we could stay."

Xander nodded in agreement. "No, go," he grumped.

"Okay," she blurted.

The two turned on their heels and dashed away, dashed away, dashed away both.

Wretchedly depressed, Giles sat down and waited for the demon prince, then abruptly stood back up. "Oh, who am I kidding?" he grumbled. "Nothing's gonna happen."

Irritably, he gathered up his equipment, checked around for anything he might have missed, and quitted the mausoleum in a huff.

A figure stepped from the shadows. "Oh, I wouldn't say that. I wouldn't say that at all. In fact, Ripper, old man, I'd say something rather interesting was about—"

The mausoleum door squeaked open, and Giles called into the gloom, "What did you s—?"

"Oh, bugger," Ethan Rayne blurted. "I'd thought you'd gone."

It was with a strange mixture of surprised delight and utter loathing that Giles said, "Ethan Rayne. You've no idea how much thrashing you is going to improve my day."

They stared at each other across the crypt. Ethan hadn't changed; he was still dark-haired and dark-eyed, square of jaw and oily of charm. Giles knew him very, very well. In days—decades—gone by, they had been part of the same coven, conjuring the forbidden forces of the darkest magicks, including a demon who had killed all the other coven members, one by one.

That demon had possessed Jenny for a time, and that

experience had caused a rift between them. Ethan had also opened a Halloween costume shop in town, cursing the costumes worn by Buffy and the others so that the demons could hold sway over the night. He had also worked for Mr. Trick and the mayor of Sunnydale, mixing up candy that changed all the adults into teenagers so that the newborn babies in the hospital nursery could be sacrificed to the one of the mayor's demonic sponsors.

And now he's back, and up to more deadly mischief, I dare say.

Ethan made a move to dart past Giles, but the Watcher was too fast for him. He tripped his erstwhile friend and sent him sprawling. Then Giles grabbed him by the collar and hauled him to his feet.

"Watch it!" Ethan protested. "Now hang on. You want to knock the crap out of me, go ahead. I can't stop you. Or, you could listen to me and find out what's going on."

Giles's hand was already pulled back, ready to deliver a punch. But he hesitated and demanded, "What are you talking about?"

"Something bad is happening. Bad for both of us," Ethan told him.

"Well, bad for you, yeah," Giles retorted.

Ethan frowned. "No, no. You have to listen. You're going to need time to prepare."

Against his better judgment, Giles did not beat Ethan to a pulp. Instead, he allowed himself to be persuaded to go the Lucky Pint, a local bar that had once been a Chinese restaurant. It retained the garish trappings of jade and scarlet lanterns and spiny dragons curled about the columns, over which was laid a veneer of British pub. Perhaps the owner imagined it to be something very Hong Kong-like, which it was not. As odd as it was, it remained the only place in Sunnydale that could make a decent Black and Tan, as they had Guinness on tap. So there he took Ethan, and the old boy stared at the scenery with such a look of dazed astonishment that Giles felt homesick for London, where the pubs were splendidly British and if one wanted Chinese, one visited a luxurious establishment such as the sublime Mr. Kai's of Mayfair.

Their waitress, attractive in a faded-rose kind of way, put down their pints and moved off. Ethan admired her retreat, then sampled his pint, clearly approving of it. Then smiled across the table at Giles and said, "Brilliant. Now, isn't this more fun than kicking my arse?"

Giles was on his guard. There had been far too many surprises of late, and he had grown weary of them.

He said firmly, "No."

Ethan looked a bit dashed. "Oh. Well, it's more fun for me."

"Just tell me what you want to tell me," Giles ordered. He felt a bit better, the merest patch more in his element, and he heard it in his own tone of voice.

Ethan pursed his lips and sighed. "Oh, so cross. We used to be friends, Ripper. When'd all that fall apart?"

"Same time you started worshiping chaos," Giles told him, although truth be told, he had paid obeisance to those dark forces as well. But he'd given it up, and returned to the good side of the force, as it were. Ethan hadn't.

Ethan looked pained as he regarded his drink. "Ahh. Religious intolerance. Sad, that. I mean, just look at the Irish troubles—"

Irritated with Ethan's flippant tone, and suddenly aware that the man was wasting his time, Giles got up to leave.

"Hang on," Ethan chided him. "I'll tell you."

Feigning reluctance, Giles sat back down. But his

ploy had worked, and now Ethan would get down to business.

The other Brit leaned forward, all serious purpose. He said, "Something's happening in the dark worlds. It's always been rumors and whispers out there. Only thing coming through clear is that something is harming demons and it's not the Slayer. You know anything about it?"

Giles ducked the question. He asked casually, "What are they saying?"

"You know demons," Ethan said, shifting in the booth. "It's all exaggeration and blank verse. 'Pain as bright as steel,' that kind of thing." He shrugged. "They're scared. And there's something called three-fourteen's got 'em scared most of all. The kind of scared that turns to angry."

Now Giles was interested. Now there was a reason to sit here and listen to this old trickster, rather than beat him to a pulp.

"Three-fourteen," Giles said. "What's that?"

Ethan shrugged. "I know we aren't particularly fond of each other, but we are a couple of old mystics."

He leaned forward. "This new outfit, it's blundering into a place it doesn't belong. It's throwing the worlds out of balance, and that's beyond chaos, mate. We're headed, quite literally, for one hell of a fight."

It's a good fight, Buffy thought as she delivered a well-placed fist to Riley's head. They sparred on the varnished wood floor in the school gym, surrounded by mirrors and exercise mats. *And no, I haven't ever had a weirder date.*

His sneakers squeaking, Riley blocked her attack, then responded with a slow-speed punch that Buffy easily ducked. No one was officially keeping score, and there was no referee. But the outcome mattered, and Buffy knew it.

As for her opponent, he looked good in sweats, and he looked good sweaty. She liked the sheen on his forehead and his forearms. He was in great shape, and his eyes were serious and intense. He tracked her like a hawk, went for the body blows and the blocks with reflexes to be proud of, and generally kept her hopping. As things got more serious, he became more agile, catching her around the neck with his arm, attempting to pull her into a headlock. She spun out of it, knocking his legs from under him. He hit the ground rolling, coming up into a wrestler's stance.

This is even better than ice-skating, Buffy thought. *Not as good as hot chocolate, but . . .*

Grinning suspiciously at her, Riley asked, "Are you holding back?"

Like him, she was panting and sweaty, and having a good time. She countered, "Are you?"

Riley kept smiling and he didn't miss a beat. "Maybe a little."

Busted. She managed the merest hint of a shrug without letting down one iota of her guard as she conceded, "Maybe a little, too."

Taking that in, his eyes flashed with interest and challenge. "I'll go all out if you will."

"You sure?" she asked, looking straight into his gaze, and what she saw there was like getting strapped in to a ride at Magic Mountain, the kind that made you barf if you ate lunch beforehand. There was a moment where you thought, *Hey wait a minute,* but you knew it was going to be so much fun that you had to go through with it.

Riley announced, "Here we go."

He pushed her back, out of his grasp. They really

went for each other, fast, hot, extreme, but Buffy mostly blocked his many forceful attacks. Then she did one simple kick; it caught Riley in the chest and blew him back ten feet. He hit the wall and collapsed to the floor. A heavy blue workout mat slammed on top of him, revealing only his feet.

"Riley!" Buffy cried. She ran to him and helped him up, asking unhappily, "Are you hurt?" She was horribly embarrassed.

He checked for broken ribs. "I . . . I'm . . . I don't think so."

She felt terrible. "I didn't . . . I'm so sorry. I didn't mean to—"

"It's fine. I'm good." He smiled at her, impressed. Buffy smiled back.

But inside, she wondered, *Is he going to be okay with this?*

Giles was drunk on good British ale, and that put him in the mind of Oxford once more, where he had been reading the classics until he went down to London and started dabbling in the occult. He had known he was to be a Watcher and couldn't bear the thought that his destiny was already planned. As far as he was concerned, all that talk about free will had been nothing more like hot air, than that spouting by the soapbox politicians spouting off in Hyde Park.

"You know what gets me?" he asked, slurring his words and not giving a bloody damn. "Here's what gets me. Twenty years I've been fighting demons. Maggie Walsh comes in, six months later, demons are pissing themselves with fear. They never even noticed me."

Ethan was drunk, too. His head wobbled as he asked Giles, "Who's Maggie Walsh?"

"Oh, she's awful," Giles said, the drinks loosening

his tongue. He gave his evil old mate an offhanded wave that said volumes about what he thought of the harridan. "Said I was an absent role model. Absent, my ass. And I'm *twice* the man she is."

"Y'know, you're really very attractive," Ethan said, and it took Giles a startled moment to realize he was talking to their waitress, who had returned to either fetch some more drinks or else tot up the bill.

"Here, luv. M'name and number," the sorcerer said, scribbling something down on his napkin. He handed it to her. "Ring me up. I'll show you a time."

"Sure." The waitress glanced at the napkin and walked off, trailing rejection in her wake. Ethan did not appear to notice, and Giles could have cared less about his prospects with the barmaid. Still, in his day, the birds flocked to Ethan, not the other way around. He'd had his pick, wherever they went. All that dark hair, that wildness . . .

Good Lord. Ethan looks positively middle-aged, he thought. *Do I look that old?*

"We've gotta face it," Giles said. "We've changed." He suppressed a beery belch. "Well, *you're* still self-centered and sadistic."

Ethan smiled goofily and raised his glass. "Here's to me!"

They clinked and drank. Giles continued, "But the world's passed us by. Someone snuck in and took us away and left these old men in our place. Clouts. Has-beens."

Ethan looked mournful. And wrinkled. Giles remembered the time Ethan had been asked to pose for a male fashion magazine; how they'd all teased the lad, though Giles had been rather envious of the other man's good looks.

"We're relics, mate," Giles continued, feeling

markedly creaky and sorry for himself. "Dusty scraps of a world that doesn't exist anymore. I mean, the bleeding 'Initiative'—their methods may cause problems, but they're getting it done. What am I? An unemployed librarian with a tendency to get knocked on the head and a drawer full of grotty amulets. 'S pathetic."

Ethan suddenly appeared stone sober. His smile vanished, and in a clear, dark voice, he leaned forward slightly and said, "You don't have to worry about all that anymore, mate. When you went to the loo I slipped a small pellet of poison in your drink. You'll be dead in an hour."

Giles stared in horror at his drinking companion. Then Ethan brayed and announced merrily, "Just kidding!"

Giles blinked, then laughed along with him. They drank. Heartily, as in the old days of pub crawling and summoning up dark forces, planning their futures and dreaming their dreams.

"I'm gonna feel like hell in the morning," Giles confided.

Ethan's face fell again. His dark eyes flashed. He said, "Yes, you will." Then, drunk again, he blatted, "Kidding!" He sat back, snickering to himself. He was extremely pissed, in the British sense of the word. "Relax. Stop thinking so much and enjoy the night. We're a couple of sorcerers. The night is still our time. The time of magick."

"To magick," Giles assented, raising his glass.

They drank.

Tara lived alone at UC Sunnydale. When she first arrived at school, she had set to work, spraying the walls black and plotting the progressions of the stars on the uneven night sky. She added webs of colored string to the astrological charts she created, and stocked her bookshelves with books on the Craft and supplies she bought at the magic shop on Main Street. Away from the influence of her family, she was free to blossom as a witch.

But now she was not alone.

Willow was actually there, in Tara's room, and Tara was so very happy. Her face was warm, and she was too shy to tell the pretty redhead that she had prayed to the Goddess for her dear new friend to come to her. And magickally, wonderfully, here she was.

Now, as Tara made a symbol on the floor with salt and black sand, Willow placed a single red rose in the center of the symbol. She looked shy and eager . . . rather the way Tara felt at this moment.

"I'm glad you wanted to get together," Willow said warmly. "I know it's late."

"I . . . thanks," Tara managed, actually getting all the words out without stammering. "I was happy you called." *Actually, I was ecstatic. I hurried to place an apple for the Goddess in the woods by the bike path.*

"We'll start out slow," Willow told her, taking the lead, and Tara was happy to let her. She very much wanted to please Willow. She couldn't wait to work a spell together.

Tara bobbed her head. "Okay."

They sat cross-legged, facing each other. At Willow's gesture, they joined hands—Tara felt the pleasant energy flowing over her skin—and closed their eyes. It was very nice, and Tara's lips bowed into a gentle smile. As they both took a breath, Tara expectantly raised her chin.

They breathed together.

Then Tara said, "Willow?"

Willow replied, "Yeah?"

"Start out slow doing what?"

They opened their eyes in unison. Willow looked a

trifle abashed, and Tara wanted to do anything to set her at ease.

"Oh, we're going to float the rose," Willow informed her. "Then use the magicks to pluck the petals off one at a time. It's a test of synchronicity. Our minds have to be perfectly attuned to work as a single delicate instrument."

Tara was filled with anticipation and joy. It sounded like an awesome spell, and it spoke volumes of the way Willow approached the Craft—with respect and gentleness, and a desire to celebrate the beauty in the Goddess' creation, which was Mother Earth. *I really like this person,* Tara thought . . . *She's sweet and nice and . . . and I think she wants to be my friend.*

"Cool," she said simply, to hide her rush of emotion. She didn't want to frighten Willow off by appearing too eager. Willow had lots of friends. She might not know what it felt like to be lonely, and to really, really want someone to hang out with. Especially someone as extraordinary as Willow. Someone who was special, unique.

"And it should be very pretty," Willow added.

Once more, they closed their eyes. Tara focused on the golden cord that attached her spirit to her body, sending waves of energy down the connection of all life and magick to her essence of her being, expanding and moving through her and from her, to the smooth, velvety soft skin of Willow's hands. The redhead's grip was strong and welcoming, and Tara's heart sang as their magicks joined and grew. She felt a warm glow as her hair blew in a swirling breeze. She thought of the old Bible verse her father had insisted she learn, to ward off the inevitable demonic possession that plagued all the female members of her family:

"Surely goodness and mercy shall follow me all the days of my life. . . ."

Tara opened her eyes, to see the rose floating above

their heads. She was so very pleased. "It worked," she said.

Willow beamed at her. "Now the hard part . . . the petals . . ."

Suddenly the rose took off, zinging around the room, bouncing off the walls and ceiling, petals flying. Both girls jumped to their feet, and they ducked a couple of times to avoid the little missile.

Zing . . . zing . . . finally it landed at Willow's feet, a battered, smoking stem. Puzzled, Willow picked it up.

"What the heck was that?" Willow asked, bewildered.

Tara was equally mystified. "I don't know." Then she added brightly, "But the petals are off."

Oh, God, I'm getting old, Giles thought. *Time was, I could drink all night and start a full day with just a cat-nap, and fare none the worse for it.*

The sunshine pierced his eyelids and the twitter of little birds penetrated his skull as if a ring of woodpeckers were drilling holes into his brains.

Groaning, he threw back the covers and almost threw himself out of bed. He trudged down the stairway, feeling incredibly heavy and clumsy, and headed for his mirror at the landing to assess the damage. *Dark circles,* he figured. *Bags and wrinkles. I shall be shocked at how old I look.*

But what he actually saw was far more shocking.

The face that reflected back at him was not that of an aging man with a hangover. It wasn't even a man's face. It was barely a face.

And what there was of that face was monstrous: It was enormous and scaled, a leathery, grotesque conglomeration of inhuman features set in an elongated head rather like that of the Alien in those films by Ridley Scott.

His oversized ears were tufted, and large, thick horns like those of a ram curled around the face.

With shaking hands he explored his features, distressed to realize that the nightmarish creature in the glass was doing the same. It was he, and no mistake.

I'm a demon?!

"No," he insisted.

Teetering in shock, he leaned in closer, squinting at the horror he had become. He reached out a hand to balance himself and accidentally punched a hole into the wall. "Oh!" he cried.

He hurried down the last few steps into his living room, still swaying, snapping the last few feet of banister off with his leathery hand as he tried to keep upright on his strange, horned hooves.

"Damn!" he shouted as he tossed the wood impatiently aside. The projectile knocked over a chair and broke it.

"*Ethan . . .*" he growled, balling his clawed hands.

Of course the sorcerer had done this; despite his assurances last night that he was teasing about putting something in Giles's drink, he *had* worked some kind of magick on his former pub-crawling mate.

I will get him for this, he vowed as he grabbed up his phone and crushed the receiver in his hand. Then he gave up and headed for the door, intent on finding Ethan and forcing him to reverse whatever spell he had performed to transform Giles into a hulking creature . . . *with goat feet!*

He grabbed up last night's shirt and began to put it on, wincing as it tore in two on the spiny ridges of his shirt. "And I liked that shirt!" he wailed.

Dropping the tatters of fabric, he grabbed the blanket off the back of his sofa and headed out the door. As he yanked it off the hinges, it fell cock-eyed against the wall.

Ethan, you're a dead man, he thought, growling.

Actually growling. Then he realized that if he killed Ethan, he would no doubt remain a demon for the rest of his existence.

It would be almost worth it, he thought.

Morning had broken, and it was a glorious new day. The local UC Sunnydale caf, the Rocket, was bustling with breakfasting students. The delicious smells of coffee and bacon permeated the air. Everyone was friendly and nicely dressed, and the sun was that big golden ball of sunshine California was known for.

Life is extremely good, Buffy thought happily. She regarded her and Willow's meals, and said, "I like pancakes 'cuz they're stackable. And waffles 'cause you could put things in the little holes if you wanted to."

Willow smiled fondly at her. "You should always have a new boyfriend. You're so fun right now."

Mildly embarrassed, Buffy smiled at her buddy. Then she changed the subject. "Hey, I didn't even hear you come in last night. Where were you?"

"The chem lab, by myself." Willow looked a bit thoughtful. "I was trying this new spell. Floating a rose. " She used her fork to demonstrate. "When all of a sudden, zing! zing! All over the room, like a . . . rose-based missile."

Buffy raised her brows. "Yikes."

Willow nodded. "I know. I think there's something out there. I felt, like, this presence, this dark-magicks energy blocking the spell. It's new."

Buffy pondered what Willow was saying. "Someone else doing magicks?"

Willow shrugged. "Maybe. If so, it's someone pretty powerful."

"Mmm. I'll tell Giles about it." Buffy brightened. "Or maybe I'll tell Maggie. She seems interested in this kind of stuff, learning the mystical biz of the demon-hunting biz."

"Tell Giles," Willow suggested. "He's feeling a little hurt right now." She cocked her head and added, "How come you never told him about Riley being a commando?"

"I did." Buffy looked a trifle confused. "I didn't?"

Willow moved into soothing mode, but she didn't fib. "He says no. He's feeling all neglected and out-of-the-loopy." She wrinkled her nose, a time-honored Willow mannerism designed to take the sting out of her words.

"Huh." Buffy did a jog down memory lane and confirmed Willow's diagnosis. She had not told Giles about Riley. That was a bit of a blunder, all right. "I mean, at first I didn't tell 'cause Riley said not to. Then, meow, cat out of the bag, and I just forgot he didn't know." She bobbed her head, indicating her journey toward decision mode. "I'll make it right . . . next time I see him. Tomorrow." *Major decision mode target has been accomplished. All systems go.* She could feel herself beaming as she confided in her girlie bud, "I'm spending today with Riley."

Willow grinned at her. "Oh, yeah. I forgot that's what you always do on days when the earth rotates."

"It's just going so well right now," she told her very best friend in the whole good world. They had shared confidences about guys for years, in their bedrooms, at the Bronze, the Espresso Pump, and now here. "I think. I hope." Her smile wilted a little. "I sort of kicked him across the room last night."

She waited for Willow's reaction, and it occurred to her, not for the first time, that Willow had a great future as a psychologist. 'Cause even though the redhead couldn't hide her alarm, she didn't act totally freaked out. Instead, she said, "Um, that's not good," just like a therapist whose patient told her she'd murdered her parents.

She'd also make a great priest, Buffy thought. *Except, okay, not a guy. But other than that . . .*

"We were sparring," Buffy explained. *Da-dumdum, punchable punch line.* "He told me not to hold back. I think he's okay with it. He's a little dented. He said he was okay with it." Now she was getting worried again. She scrunched up her face. "You think he's okay with it?"

"I'm sure he is," Willow assured her. "And even if he's not, you had to do it. I mean, he's right. You can't go around pretending you're less than you are. It wouldn't be right for you to hold back."

"Right . . . ," Buffy said uncertainly.

"What?" Willow asked, cueing in on the fact that there was more to the story than Buffy had shared so far.

Buffy was not eager to confess, but she did. "I held back a little."

Giles ran a veritable gauntlet of screaming people as he clopped along on his cloven hooves from his home to Xander's basement. He let himself in and looked around for the young man. To the offense of his British sensibilities, Xander was still wadded up in the covers on his sofa bed.

"Still asleep?" Giles muttered. "It's ten-thirty in the morning."

He stomped over to Xander's inert form and shook him by the shoulder. Gently, lest he rip off his arm.

"Xander? Xander, wake up."

Xander rolled over with his eyes still closed and muttered, "Mom?"

"No, not Mom. Now, when you look at me, you may be a little . . . alarmed," Giles said slowly and carefully. "But there's no need. It's me, Giles. Ethan has turned me into a demon, and I need your help."

Xander sleepily opened his eyes, stared at Giles, and froze.

"Hello," Giles said. "Yes, it's me."

"Yaaaa!" Xander yelled, scrambling backwards up and over the sofa. He was terror-stricken.

"Listen," Giles urged. "Can't you understand me?"

Xander was stirring, and his blurry dream images were not of Jennifer Lopez, as he had thought. They were of an incredibly ugly monster . . .

. . . zzzzz . . .

. . . that just wouldn't go away . . .

Okay, no more junk food before bedtime, or during bedtime, or when I'm asleep, and . . . Yaaaaa! There's a demon in my bedroom! For real! I am not asleep!

Hoofed and horned, the invader was hideously ugly, definitely evil, and bent on death and mayhem as it pawed violently at the air. It was the stuff of nightmares, not dreams, with bad teeth, bloodshot eyes, devil-like horns, and a really gross body roped with leathery flesh. And its eyes . . . there was no intelligence there, only a relentless need to tear and destroy.

Then it threatened him, growling, "Rrr. Grrbch fffa-har lagggh!"

"Demon! Demon!" Xander cried.

"Grbr aachjk blah!" the demon growled.

Xander raced to the shelves near his bed and grabbed a saucepan. He hurled it at the monster and grabbed another. The demon fought back, stealthily dodging the projectiles, flailing and knocking things everywhere, breaking stuff and making a huge mess as it no doubt prepared its counterattack. Xander kept throwing. Finally it turned its big, icky, spiny tail and ran away.

"That's right!" Xander shouted. "Run for your life!"

Giles escaped outside and fled through Xander's neighborhood. He darted through the gardens of the small houses. A man with a leaf blower stopped and stared, then backed up in fear. A woman carrying groceries from her car dropped the sacks in utter terror. A small child shrieked until its mother scooped it up, shouting, "Call nine-one-one!"

The turmoil and tumult were overwhelming, and Giles was in fear of his life. Americans, after all, owned and used guns. . . . "Bloody humans," he growled.

It was night. The gang had assembled on campus, sans Riley, who, Buffy supposed, was not yet actually part of the gang, and Xander was telling them about his inhuman wake up call. They were on their way to tell Giles all about it so he could do the research and save the day, as usual.

"So it had pointy things?" Buffy echoed as they marched down the street. "What kind of pointy things?"

"The pointy kind," Xander explained, keeping pace with her, but with difficulty. "And tufty ears. Oh, and it might have a saucepan-shaped bruise," he added helpfully.

"Giles'll know what it was," Willow said confidently.

But Buffy was not listening. She had just spotted Giles's front door. It was splintered and thrown off the hinges, and alarms and sirens were ringing inside her head.

Oh, my God, something's attacked Giles's place.

She walked quickly ahead and pushed open the broken door, which slid against the wall. "Giles?" she called.

Xander ran upstairs while Willow, Buffy, and Anya looked around downstairs, noting the presence of many broken items.

"Looks like Xander isn't the only one who got a visit today," Buffy said uneasily.

Xander returned down the tiled staircase. "He's not upstairs," he announced.

"Oh, God, Giles," Willow said anxiously, her voice rising with fear.

"Okay." Buffy spoke up to calm the growing anxiety filling up the room. "There's a demon, and Giles is gone." She almost faltered after she said the words, but she kept going. "But it doesn't mean that Giles is hurt. I mean, there's no blood anywhere. It might've just taken him somewhere. . . ."

She trailed off as Anya picked up Giles's ruined shirt. Buffy recognized it; it was one of the Watcher's favorites.

"I think it ate him up," Anya observed.

Buffy's knees turned to water. No one else looked much better off.

Oh, God, Giles, Buffy thought, echoing Willow's fearful cry.

It was night, and it was a cemetery, and Giles had found sanctuary from the maddened crowds. He rather understood why demons tended to congregate among the dead. Decomposing corpses had better things to do than throw pots at one and scream for police intervention.

He rounded a corner and found himself next to Spike, of all creatures that go bump in the night. The white-haired vampire was holding up a measuring tape to the side of a crypt, looking at it appraisingly. He turned, saw Giles, and smirked quite evilly.

"Well, what do I spy with my little eye?" Spike said aloud. "A demon. That would be . . . oh, right . . . the things I can kill."

During the most recently averted apocalypse, when Buffy had literally dived into the hellmouth, Spike had learned an interesting thing: that while the chip the Initiative had surgically placed in his head prevented his hurting human beings, it did nothing to stop him from harming fellow demons. This had placed him in the very astounding position of actually *wanting* to help in the fight against evil, not because the chip had transformed him into a moral creature, but so he could took his aggressions out on something, anything.

He began circling Giles in a predatory manner that made Giles sigh heavily and mutter, "Spike. *Wonderful.* The perfect end to a perfect day."

Spike's brows shot up. He said in an incredulous manner, "Giles?"

Giles flexed his muscle-y, demony arms. "Go on, then," he growled. "Let's get on with the fighting." Then he finally processed what Spike had called him. You understand me?"

"Of course I understand you," Spike said, with some amusement and a soupçon of irritation.

"I'm speaking English?" Giles asked, shocked. *Perhaps Ethan's spell has begun to wear off, and I'm becoming human again.*

But then Spike said, "No. You're speaking Fyarl. I happen to speak Fyarl." He gave Giles the once-over. "And, by the way, why the hell are you suddenly a Fyarl demon? What, you just come over all demony this morning?"

Giles said indignantly, "Matter of fact, I did. Thanks to Ethan Rayne. You've got to help me find him. He must undo this. Then he needs a good being-killed."

Spike leaned against the mausoleum and lit a cigarette. The flash from his match cast a white shadow on his white skin. He drawled, "And I'm supposed to just help you out of the evilness of my heart?"

Giles struck a threatening pose. "You-you help me and I don't kill you."

Spike was amused. "Oh, tremendously convincing. Try it again without the stutter."

"Money," Giles realized. "I could pay you money."

Spike stood up straight and tossed his cig. With an insinuating drawl, he said, "Ooh. I like money. How much?"

Giles was feeling generous. Also, desperate. "A hundred dollars."

"A hundred dollars?" Spike was incredulous. "You have to do a *lot* better than that." He was silent for a beat. Then he said, "Two hundred."

"Fine." Giles didn't even take time to think it over.

"Right, then." Spike was clearly pleased by his hard bargaining. "What's first? I run and tell the Slayer what you've gotten yourself into?"

"No!" Giles cried. Then he lowered his voice. "When I find Ethan, I can clear this up without Buffy having to know that anything happened to me at all."

Buffy, Willow, and Anya were pulling books off Giles's shelves and shoving pictures of various demons in front of Xander. So far, they were ice-cold, and things were rapidly reaching subzero.

As Xander peered at the most recent mug shot, he said. "No . . . no . . . okay, that's a giant vulture. I'd have mentioned it if it was a giant vulture."

Willow was looking very unhappy. "Buffy, even if we figure out what kind of demon got Giles, how are we going to find it?"

Buffy said unconvincingly, "We'll figure it out." She showed another picture to Xander. "This one has tufty ears."

Then they all stopped when they heard someone rattling the broken door. Buffy was instantly on alert.

Willow asked nervously, "What was that?"

"Someone's coming in," Xander replied.

Buffy pulled a stake and moved to the side of the door. Her heart was pounding in her chest. *If it's got bits of Giles stuck to it . . . I'm not thinking that,* she insisted. *Or, like a finger hanging from its lower lip, kinda like a cigarette butt . . .*

Then the door opened, and Buffy got ready to plunge her stake directly into . . . Riley.

He stared at her. "Buffy?"

"Riley? What are you doing here?"

She stowed the stake. The handsome, corn-fed commando took a look around, then returned his gaze to the Slayer. "There were nine-one-one calls. From a couple different places. Including here."

Xander cut in, not happily, "You get nine-one-one calls?"

"We have a tap into the system," Riley answered, sounding very matter-of-fact, as if violating the civil rights of Sunnydalians was no biggie. "It flags things with possible nonhuman causes. We check 'em out. What are you doing here?" he asked Buffy.

"This is Giles's apartment," she said miserably. "He's missing. The calls . . . did anyone see what did it?"

"Negative . . . no," Riley told her. "Neighbors just heard, you know, growling, things breaking. Sounded like a struggle."

Willow was on the verge of tears. "Poor Giles."

"We'll get him back," Buffy insisted, more to convince herself than anyone else.

Riley moved and acted like recon guy, and Buffy found herself torn between thinking, *Yay, cavalry,* and *Me, Slayer, you intruder.*

"What are you working on?" he asked.

"We have . . . stuff," she answered lamely. They didn't have much. Not even as much as he did, unless one counted Xander's so-not-helpful visual description. "Pictures."

Anya was more direct, and also, more honest, when she said, "We have nothing."

Buffy looked down, trying to hide her fears as they bubbled to the surface. Riley took her by the shoulders and gazed hard into her eyes, as if he was trying to transfer his hope to her. "I'll help," he promised. "The whole Initiative. We'll do whatever you need."

Buffy was moved by the offer, the complete trust it represented. *He's a good guy,* she told herself. *He knows what he's doing. He works for Maggie Walsh, and she's no slouch.*

"Thanks," she said earnestly. "I just wish I knew what I needed. I keep thinking, 'Let's ask Giles,' and then I remember."

Looking very nostalgic, Xander added, "He'd be great right now. He'd find himself in a second. Nobody's cooler in a crisis."

Giles and Spike were in Giles's Citroën, Giles wrapped in a blanket for camouflage. Spike was grinding the gears of Giles's beloved automobile. Feeling extremely uncool in this moment of crisis, demon shouted at half-demon, "If you can't *find* third gear, don't *try* for third gear!"

Spike was perhaps too overwhelmed to properly deliver a stinging reply. "Doing my best," he railed as he tried the gearshift again, missed third again. The car lurched and rumbled. "Don't know if I'm driving this thing or wearing it."

"It's perfectly serviceable," Giles said heatedly.

Spike laughed. "Funny. Hearing a Fyarl demon say 'serviceable.' Had a couple of 'em working for me once. They're more like, 'Like to crush. Crush now?' Strong, though." He gave Giles a glance. "You won't meet a jar you can't open for the rest of your life."

Giles growled.

"What was that?" Spike demanded, intrigued. "Did you growl?"

"No," Giles lied. "Listen, about Fyarl demons . . . do I have any special powers? Setting things on fire with my sizzling eye-beams?"

Spike sniffed the way he did sometimes, when he was trying to think. "Well, you got the mucus thing."

Giles was appalled. "What? *Mucus?*"

"Paralyzing mucus, shoots out the nose, sets up fast. Hard as a rock. Pretty good in a fight."

Giles was horrified. "Are you making this up?"

"Maybe," Spike offered. "But, hey, you feel a sneeze coming on, you warn me."

Giles gestured with his demony hand. "Turn here."

Spike turned the car, and they headed on Main Street, passing the buildings of Sunnydale's downtown business district.

"Downshift!" Giles bellowed. "Downshift!"

"Calm down, will you?" Spike shot back.

"I'm not sure I can," Giles admitted. "I . . . I think I'm changing."

Spike was completely unconcerned. "Fine with me, long's you pay me."

Giles gathered his blanket around himself like a security, well, blanket. He was feeling conspicuous and wretched. "I don't like this feeling. It's a sort . . . a mindless need to destroy. This anger. Rage."

Spike's angular features softened, and his voice took on a wistful tone. "Good times. Go with it."

Giles forced himself to stay calm. "No."

"It's fun!" Spike protested, throwing him another glance instead of focusing on the road. "I can't do it. Do it for me. Let yourself go!"

As rational as any Oxford don, Giles intoned, "I refuse to become a monster because I look like a monster. I am a human being." Then he glanced out the car and saw something that badly needed to be done. *But calmly, however.* "Ooh. Stop the car."

Spike did as Giles requested. They were very near the Sun Cinema, whose lights provided a fine backdrop to the fine figure of Dr. Maggie Walsh as she walked briskly down the sidewalk.

Giles hopped out and ran at her, waving his arms, roaring like a demon maniac. The cool, collected doctor utterly lost her composure, screaming and running away.

Returning to the car, Giles managed to climb back in. He was enormously pleased with himself. "Right. Let's go," he said.

Calmly.

The gang was still in Giles's apartment, and Buffy's mind wandered to the inescapable fact that things were very different on episodic TV shows than in real life. By now, Mulder or Scully would have figured out the nature of the beast, how to kill it, and whom to call. *Ghostbusters,* she thought wistfully. *Or the Smoking Man. Anyway, whomever they called, they'd do it right now or else cut to commercial, and then do it as soon as the station got through the cosmetic ads. . . .*

Xander was staring at an itching of something called a Fyarl demon. He said emphatically, pointing, *"That's* the thing that attacked me."

Wow, Buffy thought as she moved in close with the others. *Miller time. We'll be right back with the information on how to defeat this attacking monster. . . .*

"A Fyarl demon," Willow said. "Sort of a foot-soldier type. Works for other demons lots of the time. Very strong, and—hey—" She nodded to herself— "mucus."

Buffy was grossed out. "Mucus?"

Riley's cell phone summoned him. He answered it. Buffy had seen him use it before. It was actually a cross between a walkie-talkie and a Nokia, which was very cool and high-tech. "Agent Finn. Go ahead," he said. Then he began to listen.

Buffy asked Willow, "How do I kill it?"

Willow read a couple of lines. "Silver," she responded. "A weapon made of silver."

Xander chimed in. "Did you just say 'mucus'?"

Willow said firmly, 'You don't want to know."

Still with the listening, Riley finally said, "When? Yes." Then, he distinctly looked at Buffy with something less like adoration and more like discomfort and said, "I understand."

Before Buffy could ask about the look, he disconnected the call and said, "The demon attacked Professor Walsh. It got out of a small gray car." He hesitated. "A Citroën."

Willow exclaimed, "It stole Giles's car!"

Xander was confused. "Why would a demon steal a car?"

Anya was more honest. "Why would a demon steal *that* car?"

I gotta get the gang on track, Buffy thought. *Move my troops into formation. I wonder if the Initiative has a war room, with a big, bumpy map and little wooden blocks or plastic soldiers or something to move around with those elegant little rake-things?* "A demon that steals a car has a reason. A purpose."

Everyone looked at her. Reacted to the purposeful change in her. That was of the good.

"But it doesn't sound like Fyarl demons are really big independent thinkers. Willow, the spells that have been going wrong—could that be caused by someone using magicks to control a demon? Making this Fyarl demon attack Giles?"

Willow nodded excitedly. "Yeah. Yes, that would draw a lot of dark energy."

Speaking of energy, the energy in the room shifted. There was a plan now, and the gang was looking at Buffy, waiting for orders from headquarters. *I love these guys,*

Buffy thought with a rush of feeling. *They're gonna help me find Giles.*

"Okay. Willow, Xander, stay here. Whoever's controlling the demon may call and ask for ransom. You give 'em anything they want," Buffy said.

"You got it," said dear, fantastic, wonderful Xander.

"Riley, come with me to the magick shop. Maybe they needed supplies."

She headed for the door, Riley joining her, then made a detour at Giles's desk. She scanned for silver objects. "Something silver . . ." Then, with a small thrill of victory, she grabbed a letter opener.

"A letter opener?" Riley asked, with a small dash of skepticism. "That's not very sharp."

"Then I'll have to put some muscle behind it," she replied.

She left, Riley trailing behind.

Swaddled in his blanket, Giles kept to the shadows near the end of the bar of the Lucky Pint while Spike relished his new role as an intelligence operative. Council material, the vampire was not. Giles felt as if he himself were living in the original version of *The Invisible Man,* the rather grotty one with Claude Rains.

Spike was saying to the waitress, the same one Ethan had tried to chat up, "Two of 'em. English like me, but older and less attractive. One of them gave you his phone number."

"I threw it out," the woman informed Spike. Giles sagged in defeat. Then she added, "I mean, I took one look, saw he was staying at that rattrap. No thanks."

Spike said, with utmost operative smoothness, "Which rattrap?"

"The one by the highway. The Sunnydale Motor Inn."

In a trice, they were out the door. Giles slammed it. It broke.

Soon my head will be the thing being trounced, he thought hopefully. *Just as in the old days.*

Crash.

Buffy kicked in the locked door of the magick shop. *It's a good night to be the Slayer.* The door way as if it hadn't been locked at all, and Buffy was all business as she entered the place. She looked around and found some stacks of receipts.

"Credit card slips," Buffy informed her sidekick, not of the door but of the mission. "Copies of receipts. Help me look."

Riley took some, saying, "You shouldn't have done that to the door."

Sometimes his by-the-book attitude irked her. *Just a smidge.* She casually replied, "Don't have time to play by the rules tonight."

"I have a master key," he elaborated. "Opens every shop on Main Street."

"Oh." Embarrassed, she shrugged it off, saying, "Next time. Absolutely."

Riley gestured to the receipts in his hands and said, "I don't know what I'm looking for."

Eureka. Or some other, cooler Slayer-slang. "I do." She held it up. "Ethan Rayne."

Riley looked interested. "Who's that?"

Her jaw set. There were times when the code that forbade her from killing human beings really got in her way.

"Professional bad guy," she bit off. "He's gotta be the one who made the demon go after Giles." She added, with grim satisfaction, "At least we know who we're looking for."

Riley whipped out his Double-Oh-Initiative cell

phone and barked into it, "Commander, are you there?"

"What are you doing?" Buffy demanded.

"This is Agent Finn. I need a search. Local hotel registrations matching the name Ethan Rayne." He looked at Buffy's receipt. Or rather, Ethan's. "R-A-Y-N-E," he said into the phone. "Call me back."

As he whipped it shut, Buffy exclaimed, "You can do that?"

"It'll take a couple minutes." He sounded both proud and apologetic at the same time, a not-unknown Riley tone of voice to take.

Buffy took that in and started heading for the door. "Let's get in your car. Be ready to go," she suggested.

Riley got in her way. "Buffy, earlier, when I talked to Professor Walsh? She gave me very specific orders."

Buffy was all ears. "Yeah?"

Now apologetic-voice overruled proud voice. "She said, when we located the demon, I'm not supposed to bring you along."

She copied that with a casual, "Oh." She continued heading for the door.

Riley followed.

"What are you doing?"

She half-turned, looked up at him. "I'm going to the car." There was an edge to her voice, and she was gonna keep it there, just in case. "And then we're going where the demon is."

"Buffy, I can't take you along," he insisted.

Kicking her edge-voice up a notch, she informed him crisply, "You aren't taking me with you. I'm going, and I'm letting you come with me."

"Buffy, it's not really your call." He gestured for emphasis, and she was not loving the movement of his hands and arms the way she usually did. "This is a military operation now."

Watcher
and Slayer

Giles prepares Buffy for the Cruciamentum.

Zackary Kralik

"She passed. You didn't."

Buffy and her new man:
Special Agent Riley Finn
~
Giles learns about the Initiative.

A monstrous makeover for Anthony Stewart Head.

"Demon! Demon!"

Summers' blood is thicker than magick.

"Mmmm. Righteous."

Glory searches for the key.

Rupert "Ripper" Giles

Another notch on the edginess as she said heatedly, "So get the troops to stop me, 'cause nothing less than that's gonna do it. This demon did something to Giles. And I'm gonna kill it."

There was a moment, a very short one, where she thought her boyfriend might actually throw down. Her mind flashed back to the sparring session in the school gym, and the damage she had inflicted on him even when holding back. She so did not want to hurt Riley in any way, ever.

Don't make me choose, she pleaded. *Don't ever make me choose, 'cause Giles was in my life first, and he is my Watcher.*

With grim purpose, she turned and left.

He followed.

Good. Collision course averted.

At least for now.

More with the ruining of Giles's car, as Spike ground the gears. Giles likewise ground his teeth, seated beside the vampire in the passenger's seat, no blanket in sight. He was tired of coddling these humans, hiding his frightening exterior from such inferior beings.

As he thought of what he'd like to do to the lot, he growled low in his throat.

Spike glanced over. "How're you feeling, mate?"

"Like snapping necks until everyone's dead." His voice emanated deep and guttural.

Spike was delighted. "Now *that* sounds like a Fyarl demon. Good for you." As he spoke, he glanced into the rearview mirror. "Hey, picked up a tail."

"Just a little one," Giles asserted. "Hurts to sit."

Spike bobbed his head at the mirror. "I mean, someone's following us." As Giles twisted around, he squinted into wide-set headlights on a rectangle of shadow.

"Humvee. Military." Spike spoke with the authority of someone who's run away many, many times.

"Lose them. Speed up," Giles ordered.

Spike snorted. "I've got it floored. Why'd you buy this car?"

"Do something!" Giles growled. "If they catch us, we both end up in a lab."

What Spike did was turn the wheel so sharply that the car almost skidded out of control. The bright headlights behind them traveled along with it.

"It's getting closer," Spike said unhappily. Then, more lights, as another Humvee cut in behind them at a side street. "And it's got a friend."

"Damn!" Giles shouted. In frustration, Giles put his demony hand through the passenger side window. Glass shattered.

"Sure. Dismantle the getaway car," Spike snapped at him. "That'll scare 'em."

Giles had no patience—and was perhaps losing the intellectual ability—to react to Spike's sarcasm. He said, "Slow down. I'll jump out. They'll follow you."

"Hold on." Spike was not loving the plan. "These commandos, they're the same guys that're after me, too. Maybe I want you around to split their attention a bit."

"I'll pay you another hundred dollars," Giles informed his Mr. Toad-like chauffeur.

His much-maligned Citroën immediately took a turn, slowing marginally. Giles flung opened the door, taking as much care as possible not to rip it off the hinges, and leaped from the moving vehicle. He rolled, feeling impressively macho, and also rather pleased with the prospect of ripping off the heads of any of the soldiers who might be so foolish as to get out of their Humvee and attack him.

But his car sped off, the two Humvees right behind it. His plan was successful.

He growled with hellish delight.

Giles saw the bloody bastard through the motel room window. It was, as the serving wench had said, dismissively cheap. Two double beds, a dresser, a TV, not much to work with, but he would pummel the sorcerer into a bloody pulp with whatever was handy. Including his own leathery demon paws.

Ethan was stuffing clothes into a hard-sided suitcase when Giles burst in. Ethan looked appropriately terrified to see his old mate.

"Gaaah! Giles?"

With cold menace, Giles advanced. "Found you."

Ethan backed up as if from a wild dog. "Calm down." He held out his hands in front of him. "It's okay. Good Giles."

Giles answered, unaware that what Ethan heard sounded very much like, "Vvrrooh, rrrraatha, hrrrrr!" Or syllables to that effect.

Ethan ventured, "I don't actually speak Fyarl."

Giles lunged at the blackguard. Ethan responded in typical manly fashion by ducking and running, zipping around the edge of the room, climbing over the bed, the dresser, the other bed . . .

"I can't undo it if you kill me!" Ethan cried out.

Roaring, Giles grabbed Ethan by the shirtfront and tossed him across the room. Ethan scrambled to his feet some distance away. Giles raised a hand, pressing one nostril closed, threatening. His meaning was clear:

It's mucus time.

Then Buffy and Riley burst in.

Saved! Giles exulted. *As soon as I suffocate Ethan in my bodily fluids, we'll have cake!*

"You gotta stop it!" Ethan bellowed. "It killed Ripper and now it's trying to get me!"

Giles's own slayer went for him, dealing him a flying kick that threw him back. He roared and roared again, outraged and afraid, trying to protest his innocence.

Meanwhile, Ethan tried to sneak out, but Buffy's young man blocked him. Ethan threw a punch, which the young man countered quite efficiently. Ethan wasn't going anywhere.

Giles, unfortunately, was. He was going down. Buffy was pummeling him, beating him up, beating him down. It appeared that she was planning to kill him.

Wishing there were another way to handle the situation, Giles tried to discuss things with her in Fyarl, knowing it now as the mother of his tongue, and proud, damn it, proud of his demonic heritage. He was changing, becoming even less human, and it was with very little hesitation that he threw her against a wall.

The room was a blur, as was the petite blond human, as the fight progressed. Finally, Buffy knocked him down. She looked directly at him, fire in her eyes. "What did you do to him?" she demanded. *"What did you do?"*

Think of the three hundred quid, think of the fags and blood you can buy, Spike told himself as he turned the Citroën into an alley. One of the Humvees missed the turn, and Spike was jubilant.

Leaning out of the car, and yelling at the foolish American military, he shouted, "You just try to catch me, filthy commando pigs! You just try—"

He turned to face front again in time to see that the alley was being blocked by a truck backing away from a loading dock, directly into his path.

"Oh, blast," he bit out. He spun the wheel wildly, turned, and missed the truck by inches. "Ha! Knew I could do it! Not gonna—"

Blam! Crash! Crunch! It was a lovely day to own a wrecking yard, if one had a hankering for semiusable

Citroën parts. Or pallets of squashed fruits and vegetables: Spike had rammed a loading dock loaded with goods for the morning market. The fragrance of pressed corn and pulped tomato mingled with motor oil and fuel, reminding him very much of the England of his human life, thick in the startup of IndustrialRevolution.com.

After a beat, he crawled out of the totaled Citroën, pushing the wreckage of the pallets out of his way. He took off running, yelling, "I can kill demons! *And* I can crash cars! Things are looking up!"

William the Bloody ran off into the night.

I never completely appreciated how much damage she can inflict, Giles reflected as Buffy flipped over the folding suitcase stand, picking it up as she went and clamping it down on Giles's head. She twisted it, and he roared and swatted her, knocking her to one side.

On the other hand . . .

Crush is good. Can crush now?

Buffy's young man was distracted from guarding Ethan by the fight. As he glanced over at his tumbling girlfriend, Ethan took advantage and swung. But the lad was swift in his retaliation, blocking Ethan's punch with his forearm and returning better than Ethan tried to give with his severely brutal punch at Ethan.

Crush, crush, crush, Giles thought exuberantly. *Kill.*

Then he shouted in Fyarl as he kicked at Buffy's limp body, rolling her over onto her back. He threw his head back and let loose with a chest-thrumming roar of triumph.

Buffy's eyes snapped open. She braced her arms on the floor and kicked straight up with both legs, catching Giles in the head and knocking him to the ground. She flipped onto her feet and launched herself at him, pummeling him with punches. Then she knelt on his chest and pulled something shiny from her jacket. It was his letter opener.

She pressed the tip against his throat and braced both hands on it, ready to drive it through his neck. "This is for Giles," she announced.

"For me?" he asked, confused.

She plunged the letter opener into his chest. At the same time, now face-to-face, she stared into his eyes. "Oh, God. *Giles.*"

"Yes, yes!" he cried, nodding enthusiastically, although he had no reason to believe that she spoke Fyarl.

"Oh, God!" she cried, pulling the letter opener back out. "Giles! Giles! I'm sorry! Don't die!"

He told her sincerely, "Actually, I feel quite well. Except for the rage."

Buffy said over her shoulder, "I think he's okay." She regarded the letter opener, examining it more closely. "Is this real silver?"

No, it's pewter, Giles thought. *It was a gift.*

It took very little coercion—actually, none—to persuade Ethan to do a reversal spell. Happily, he still had sufficient quantity of a number of the items he'd purchased at the magick shop to accomplish the deed, and Giles found himself none the worse for wear, except for the truly awful shirt of Ethan's that he put on once he had become human again.

Riley Finn was speaking into his walkie-talkie as Ethan muttered, "I've really got to learn to just do the damage and leave town. It's the stay-and-gloat gets me every time."

Giles said nothing, only regarded himself in the cheap mirror of the cheap motel room, assuring himself that there were no traces of demon in his features. *It would have been fun to keep the mucus,* he thought a bit wistfully.

Buffy crossed to him, looking both happy and sheepish. "Giles, you okay?" she asked.

He felt precisely the same way. "Embarrassed, mostly," he confessed. "Buffy, I don't know what to say. You know I'd never intentionally . . ." *do the things I did,* he almost added. *Except for terrorizing Walsh. That was brilliant.*

"I know," she assured him.

"How did you know it was me?"

"Your eyes." Her voice was quiet and soft, her expression the same. Then she got back a bit of her mischievousness, grinning at him. "There's only one person in the world that can look that annoyed with me."

He smiled at her. There was a moment for them, a reunion of sorts, and Giles realized that yes, the years had rolled over him and yes, he might be obsolete in many ways. But he had this young girl's heart, and her trust. Their bond had withstood this test, as it had so many others.

Her birthdays are hard on us, Giles thought. *But all's well that ends well.*

Behind them, Ethan groused, "Is this going to go on much longer? I'd rather like to be going."

Slayer smiled knowingly at Watcher. She wheeled around and regarded Ethan with disdain and skepticism, as only a newly-minted nineteen-year-old can deliver.

"Now, why would I let you go?" she drawled.

Ethan was sure he was on steady ground. "Well, maybe 'cause you have no choice. I'm human. You can't kill me. What's a slayer gonna do to me?"

It was rather like a parlor-room play as Riley ushered in two large, uniformed U.S. Military policemen. One of them handcuffed Ethan while Riley intoned, "By the authority of the U.S. Military, you are being taken into custody pending a determination of your status."

The two MPs hauled an astonished Ethan out of the motel room as Riley continued: "They'll take Mr. Rayne to a secret detention facility in the Nevada desert. I'm sure he'll be rehabilitated in no time."

That sounds distinctly splendid, Giles thought as he trailed after the trio. "If you don't mind," he said to his young people, "I'm going to go watch them manhandle him into a vehicle."

He left the room, eager to observe the proceedings.

Then, through the open door, he heard Buffy say to Riley, "Thanks."

"I told you I'd help," he replied, and Giles smiled, both at the fondness in the boy's voice, and also at the way Ethan was being forced to sit inside one of the Humvees that had unsuccessfully sought to squash him and Spike flat.

"You did," Buffy continued. "If I'd gotten here any later . . . If Giles had killed Ethan, I'd never have gotten him back."

You'd find another route, Giles thought, at the same time that Riley Finn told his slayer, "You'd find some other way."

"You're really strong," Riley said to Buffy. "Like, Spider-Man strong."

"Yes," she replied. "I don't stick to stuff, but yeah."

Perhaps we can work on that mucus thing, Giles mused. *Figure it out, give her another weapon of destruction to fling upon the forces of darkness. . . .*

"And . . . you're in charge. You're, like, make the plan, execute the plan, no one giving you orders," Buffy's lovesick swain said.

"I'm the Slayer." No pride, no boasting, just a complete acceptance and total knowing.

Brava, Buffy, Giles thought. From the back of the Humvee, Ethan scowled at him and Giles gave him a jaunty wave.

"I like it," Riley told Buffy.

"Yeah?" she asked.

There was another beat. Perhaps another kiss . . .

"But give me another, oh, week to get ready and . . . I'll take you down."

Giles raised his brows, mildly embarrassed, and moved away as the Humvee rolled away. Ethan was off on his exciting adventure into a remote desert.

Preferably, one without lots of missile silos. Ethan's awfully resourceful.

"*Ciao,* old man," Giles murmured, unable to suppress the last lingering bits of affection he had for the wily magick-user.

It was difficult to believe that only three days had passed since the eve of Buffy's surprise birthday party. But day four looked to be a lovely one, with the bright, golden glow for which California was renowned. Buffy looked on as Giles finished hooking up a new phone.

She said cheerily, "Nice phone."

"Yes. Fabulous technology," he mused aloud. "You see, if anyone has any information I need to know, they can simply tell me about it through this ingenious speaking tube. I'm very excited."

"I'm sorry, Giles. I really thought I'd told you about Riley and the Initiative." Buffy's tone was as genuine and sincere as it had been with Riley.

His phone installation completed, Giles moved around to sit in a chair near Buffy as she said, "And I know that doesn't help. I promise it won't happen again. I'll tell you everything."

"Buffy, I don't want to ask you to betray any confidence, and I certainly don't want to interfere—"

"Uh-oh. You have 'but' face." At his bewildered look, she added, "You're about to say 'but.'"

Ah. "But this . . . Initiative." He knew he needed to be as sincere and genuine with her as she had been with him.

"I'm a little concerned. Ethan's not exactly a reliable source, but I'm not sure he's wrong about them."

"I'm not dating the Initiative." She looked supremely confident, and he envied the fact that at her age there was much in the world that was still black and white. "I'm dating Riley. And he's a good guy, Giles."

"I believe that. But—" He searched for the words to convey his meaning without putting her on the defensive— "He's part of something we don't really understand."

Her grin was sly. "You sure you're not just saying that because you don't like his boss?"

"No," he insisted, "that's not what I'm saying at all . . . although I do hate her quite a lot." Buffy's grin got bigger. "I want you to have your personal life. Just . . . just keep your eyes open," he requested. "Make sure you know what you're getting into."

He saw that she understood him. He hoped that she would also listen to him.

I'd best write this all down, he thought. *Keep track of it, for posterity if for no other reason.*

He put on some water for tea, got out his journal, and began a new entry.

Beneath the frat house, Riley walked with Maggie Walsh in the secret world that was their world. Above them and beyond the secured doors of Wolf House, the sun shone and birds trilled. Civilians went about their lives, innocent of what went on down in the bowels of UC Sunnydale.

Riley was proud to help them maintain that innocence.

"So she walks in and the rules just suddenly . . . break," Professor Walsh said.

"Um . . . pretty much," Riley admitted.

She gazed at him with her intelligent eyes. She was the smartest woman—person—he had ever know. Also, the gutsiest. He admired the hell out of her.

"Be careful with her," Dr. Walsh told him. "She reacts on instinct. There's no discipline there. Her loyalties are uncertain."

"You won't be disappointed in her," Riley promised. "She's good at what she does, and—" he felt a rush of emotion "—she has the truest soul I've ever known."

Amused, Maggie Walsh rolled her eyes and chuckled. "Oh, no. Spontaneous poetic exclamations. Lord, spare me college boys in love."

Riley was not embarrassed in the least. "I'm just saying she'll work out. You'll be proud of her."

Professor Walsh regarded him. "You want to know what I think?" He waited. She smiled again and said, "I think you're probably right."

Riley left her then, walking down a hallway. Maggie stopped before a door and punched in a complex code. She entered a room and drew close to an examining table. On it was a large form beneath a sheet.

She closed the door, blocking Giles's view as he stared with Krathalal into the vision flames.

The number on the door was 314.

"She duped him even then," Giles murmured as he stared into the ring of flame surrounding himself. The pain was nigh overwhelming, but steady. He was beginning to find it extremely difficult to concentrate, and yet he understood that he must. For Buffy's sake. "He truly is an innocent."

"You are speaking of yourself," Krathalal observed. "The Slayer duped you."

"Not at all," he said, surprised.

"She cast you aside. After all you did for her."

"As she should have done," Giles said. *"She was growing up."*

The Council had accused him of caring for Buffy as a father, and he saw that that was true. Part of acting as a father figure was letting go of her, allowing her to find her own way, and he realized that he had reacted to his change in stature with natural and predictable distress and sadness.

"She stopped caring about you," Krathalal insisted. *"She almost killed you, and she would never give her life to save yours."*

Giles felt a rush of exhilaration as he realized that the demon was trying to tempt him away from their bargain, which must mean that their pact was made . . . and that Krathalal would not break his word.

"Step into the third ring of fire," Krathalal intoned. *"See what a foolish pact you're making."*

The flames seared him, inside and out. They glowed and crackled a vivid green, the color of moss on dead flesh, and Rupert Giles knew in his soul that something precious was being taken from him.

Something that in future, he would miss very much, and regret giving to this demon.

No price is too great, *he reminded himself.*

"Now, open your book. The journal that nearly caused the death of Dawn, and the unraveling of the world . . ."

Giles did so.

Read to me.

"Blood Ties"

*B*uffy and her friends were arguing about the proper way to celebrate her birthday while Giles wrote in his journal. They were hanging out in the Magick Box, which Giles owned, and he half-listened as he wrote:

I can't believe that Buffy's birthday is once again on the horizon. It seems just yesterday that we were celebrating her nineteenth, and here she is going to be twenty. Many Slayers—most—don't make it to their twentieth birthday, he thought, *feeling rush of a fierce pride and fear. Sometimes I feel as though she is living on borrowed time.*

And God strike me dead for even thinking such a thing.

So much has happened since then. I've bought the magic shop, and Anya works for me. Joyce had a terrible brain lesion, which has apparently been taken care of through surgery. Willow has found a soulmate in the young Wicca, Tara, and their exploration of magick has proven quite impressive.

But I am avoiding the most important topic, and that is Dawn, Buffy's little sister. Until recently, I was completely convinced—as was Buffy, and as the others still are—that Dawn was Buffy's younger sister, that she has always been her sister, and that there was nothing whatsoever unusual about her. But Buffy and I have deduced that Dawn is a created being. Approximately six months ago, the Monks of the Order of Dagon used Buffy's DNA to manufacture her, as it were. In reality, Dawn Summers is a powerful energy force called "the Key."

Dawn does not know this. No one knows this, save Buffy and me—and Joyce—because the knowledge is too dangerous to share. The Monks hid Dawn as well as they could, because a Hellgod named Glory has arrived in our dimension and is frantically searching for this Key. Glory wears the appearance of a lovely young woman (who dresses rather provocatively), but make no mistake: she is virtually ageless, brutal, and quite insane, and we have not yet figured out a way to prevent her doing whatever she likes. If she discovers that Dawn is the Key . . .

"Look," Buffy was saying, startling Giles from his writing, " I know Mom wants to gather and make with the merry tomorrow night, but with everything going on—"

"This is exactly what you need!" Willow insisted. "A twentieth birthday party with presents and funny hats and candles you can't blow out!" She turned to Tara and said conspiratorially, "Those used to scare me."

"Me, too," Tara told her redheaded girlfriend, and they shared one of those very sweet moments that often passed between them, then got back to the matter at hand.

"I just don't know if this is a good time to break out the party piñata, Will," Buffy persisted. "We need to stay focused if we're going to find a way to stop Glory."

Xander was still injured from his run-in with Olaf, swinger of the great hammer, and perhaps that gave him a more mature perspective. He nodded in agreement with Buffy and reminded the others, "We're going up against a god. An actual, mightier-than-thou god."

Willow was thus far unconvinced. "You know what they say. The bigger they are—"

"The faster they stomp you into nothin'," Anya cut in.

Everyone looked at the former vengeance demon. As he resumed his writing, Giles thought to himself, *She's taken the place of Cordelia as the one who says the uncomfortable truths. And also, healed Xander's heart in the process. Why does he attract the demons so?*

Buffy nodded in Anya's direction. "She's right. I've thrown everything I've got at her, and she just shrugs it off."

"Then we have to find something heavier to throw," Willow asserted.

Giles looked up from his notes.

"That might pose some difficulty. From what the Council has been able to discover from the *Book of Tarnis* and other sources, Glory and two of her fellow Hellgods ruled one of the particularly nastier demon dimensions."

Buffy looked less than overjoyed by his statement. She wrinkled her forehead as she asked, "There's more than one?"

"There are thousands of demon dimensions. All different," Anya said helpfully. No one else appeared to feel particularly . . . helped.

"And all pushing at the edges of this reality, trying to find a way in," Giles added.

"I guess Glory found one," Buffy responded. "The question is why?"

Giles shrugged. *The* Book of Tarnis *thus far has not*

answered that most vexing question, he wrote. He looked up and said, "There's nothing to indicate that, so far. Just vague references to chaos and destruction."

Willow sighed. "Just once I'd like to hear a reference to balloon animals."

Buffy remained on task. "Okay, so we know where Glory's from, but what do we know about her? She's tough, yeah, but no bolts of lightning or blasts of fire. Shouldn't a god be able to do that kind of stuff?"

"Usually, yes," Giles told her, pushing up his glasses. "Being in human form must be severely limiting her powers. All we have to worry about now is her being immortal, invulnerable, and on the constant brink of insanity."

"A crazy Hellgod," Xander said, sighing. "And the fun just keeps on leaving."

"Being human is affecting her mental capacity," Giles elaborated. "The only way she's been able to keep her mind intact is by feeding off the energy of human brains."

Tara was horrified. She ducked her head in her gentle way and murmured, "She—she's a brain sucker?"

Giles wished he could reassure Tara . . . reassure all of them. But they had come too far as a group, gone through too much, for him to prevaricate. They had always been strong enough to hear the truth, and he was profoundly proud of all of them . . . *especially Buffy.*

"She absorbs the energies that bind the human mind into a cohesive whole," he explained, warming to his task. "But once drained, all that's left behind—"

"Are crazy people," Buffy finished, comprehending the situation entirely.

"At least vampires just kill you," Tara said weakly. Willow regarded her with compassion. Like Buffy, Willow had matured in a marvelous way. He could scarcely recall the stammering, insecure girl he had first met at Sunnydale High.

"We have to come up with something to stop her," Buffy insisted.

"Tara and I could work on some tactical spells," Willow suggested. "If she's not too punchable, maybe she's not totally invulnerable to magick."

The others at the table—Xander, Anya, Willow and Tara—rather cheered up at that, as did Buffy, who had begun pacing. She said, "That's a start."

"I can help with the research," Anya offered, waving her fingers as if she were raising her hand in class. "I know way more about demon dimensions." Giles huffed, and she said, "Well, I do."

"This is all great long-term plan-y stuff," Xander piped up, "but what about this Key thingy Glory's looking for?"

There was a distinct sense of moving on to new business as Tara agreed, saying, "Yeah. Shouldn't we be trying to find it before she does?"

Oh, dear. Giles traded looks with Buffy.

"I don't think we have to worry about that," Buffy said evasively. And Giles relaxed, sure the group would content themselves with that answer.

But he was wrong.

Willow frowned, sitting up slightly in her chair. "They've got a point. Whatever Glory's planning on opening with the Key, I'm guessing it won't be filled with flowers and candy."

"So where do we start looking?" Xander asked, addressing the group at large. "Do we know where it used to be kept? Who saw it last—"

Giles watched Buffy, willing to take his cue from her. Discovering the truth about Dawn had been a terrible shock, one they had agreed to share between themselves—and Joyce. It had been almost impossible to "wrap one's head around it," as they loved to say nowadays.

Giles knew that once the others knew that Dawn was the key, the revelation would distract them, take up valuable time. On the other hand . . .

"We did," Buffy said, looking as uncomfortable as he. "Giles and me. We know where it is, so—"

There was movement all round the table. Xander's eyes got enormous, and he blurted indignantly, "You *what?!*"

"You know and you didn't tell us?" Willow echoed, likewise astonished and dismayed.

Giles felt he ought to say something. He leaned forward. "There were reasons."

"If Glory found out you knew where it was . . . I didn't want to put you in that kind of danger." Buffy's words sounded like the weakest of rationalizations, and Xander gave his head a little shake.

"As opposed to the other kind we're always in? Glory's going nuts trying to get her hands on the Key, and you've known where it is all along?" he accused.

Oh, dear. They're not going to give up. It's that indomitable American spirit, I'm afraid. Yanks never could take no for an answer . . .

"You should have told us," Willow agreed, hurt and angry.

"Willow . . ." Buffy paused. Giles watched her mind working, observed her decision-making process. Her shoulders slumped and she exhaled, and he knew what was coming next.

"You're right." Softly, to Giles, she said, "It's time."

He spoke equally softly, although of course the others could hear him. "Are you sure?"

She sighed again and gestured to the others. "They're going to be risking their lives. They deserve to know."

Something in her expression convinced him; he was glad of it, really. Keeping secrets from Americans was always difficult. They hadn't the sense of decorum British people did, they simply bumbled into a situation demanding to know what was going on, as if it were one of their famous inalienable rights.

As if to underscore his contention, Xander pushed. "Know what?" he demanded.

Buffy steeled herself. Giles sat at the ready in case she needed his support in a more overt manner.

Here we go, he thought, and Buffy said carefully, "There's something I have to tell you. About Dawn."

Yes, she's right, Giles thought. *It's time.*

God help us, every one.

Surrounded by the blue borealis of mystical energy, Orlando knelt with the other Knights of Byzantium around the campfire. The woods outside Sunnydale were dark and deep, and as he prayed with their others he gave thanks for this excellent hiding place, where they could perform their rituals and prepare themselves for their quest . . . to find and destroy the Key.

His mind shifted from their holy chant to the thought that he might very well die here, in the small American town of Sunnydale—the cursed place where the Order had sent the Key. He did not mind perishing for the cause—he would be proud to do so—and he supposed Sunnydale was the place for it. He sensed that the final battle would be here.

With the others, he held his inverted sword to his forehead like a makeshift cross, and joined in the rite.

"The link must be severed. Such is the will of God. The Key is the link. The link must be severed. Such is the will of God."

Then someone spoke outside the group, and not with friendly words:

"You really think He's going to help you?"

Orlando and the other knights leaped to their feet, swords at the ready. It was one of the Hellgod's minions, an ugly, troll-like being with pointed ears, standing at the outskirts of the camp. His face was bruised, and his smile was warm.

"I fear your faith is gravely misplaced," the minion continued.

Five more of its kind burst from the surrounding woods and attacked. Wielding halberds, they rushed the knights, who met the challenge with honor.

The battle began. Steel flashing, swords clanging, men grunting with agony. The blue light cast eerie shadows on the faces of the wounded, the fading gazes of the dying.

Orlando ducked and rolled, narrowly avoiding having his head cut off by one of the disgusting creatures. His fellow knight Morded deflected a sword thrust and knocked his attacker out cold with the hilt of his sword, then immediately pulled the blade back, skewering the minion behind him.

Edward, Orlando's oldest friend among the band, dropped to the ground, kicking the legs out from under his assailant, and ran the troll through the heart.

On his feet, Orlando sidestepped another minion's halberd thrust, timing it so that the blade impaled another of the enemy—an old trick. It seemed that all the old tricks worked on this motley band. Then he punched his original attacker, knocking him unconscious before it hit the ground.

The leader of the minions stood alone, staring incredulously at the sight of the five henchtrolls, downed and neutralized. Orlando allowed himself a smile as he wiped his sword and advanced on the creature. "Shall we test your faith now?" he asked the minion.

The creature turned to flee, stumbled, fell. He sucked

in air as Orlando brought his sword down for the death blow—

—but Orlando's sword was stayed an inch from the minion's fleshy head by a feminine hand with lacquered red nails.

The hand belonged to Glory the Hellgod.

Orlando's terror nearly overcame him. Here was the god he had sworn to oppose until his death, grinning up at him in her guise as a beautiful human woman dressed in scarlet.

"Never send a minion to do a god's work," Glory drawled.

She backhanded Orlando, sending him flying. The knights attacked, swords flashing; in a blur, Glory deflected the blows with her bare hands, crushing Orlando's men with frightening ease. Morded, Edward, Pieter, Roland—all went down, leaving him alone to face the beast.

Barely conscious, he spotted his sword and reached for it . . . but Glory reached it first. "Hey, nice sword," she said, smiling brightly at him, admiring the razor-sharp weapon.

The link must be severed, he chanted silently, preparing himself for death. *The Key is the link . . .*

"Bet it hurts," the god trilled at him.

It did.

But only briefly.

It was afternoon in Sunnydale, and as was often the case in the deceptively innocuous town, the golden sunshine assured everyone that they would enjoy a beautiful day. Hedges surrounded attractive California bungalow-style cottages and larger Arts and Crafts homes. Skateboarders cruised wide boulevards, and frisky pups barked at them as they passed.

Sprinklers chattered on, skittered off, and no one knew—or acknowledged—that beneath all the Pleasantville, Technicolor horror was weaving webs that would, by nightfall, suck the soul out of a few lives here, a few there, while the rest of the population went about their business.

Willow and Tara were marking runic symbols on the sidewalk around the perimeter of Giles's store. Typical Sunnydale that no pedestrians took much notice, except for one sweet-looking old lady, who smiled and reminisced about her hopscotch days before announcing to the two witches that she was on her way to the sporting goods store to buy herself a new handgun.

Then Dawn bounced up, backpack hanging so normally on her, well, back, fresh from school and ready for hanging out.

"Hey! You guys doin' a spell?" she asked, very chipper and very . . . Dawn.

Willow did a kind of mental stumble, and tried to cover, quickly.

"Dawn, hey," she said, hearing herself sound breathy. "Yeah, it's an early warning incantation. If anything Hell-god-ishly powerful comes within a hundred feet of the shop, screechy siren things'll, you know, screech."

Tara nodded earnestly. "That should give us enough of a heads-up to hide—" *whoa, slow down,* Willow begged, but Tara was already there— "the, uh, Key."

"We already put one up around your house," Willow added, then wondered if that was saying too much. *Yikes. It feels like saying, "Hi" is saying too much.*

"Cool," Dawn chirped, oblivious to their internal hiccups. "Can I help?"

Willow and Tara looked at each other, and if looks could talk, which they could . . .

"I don't think Buffy would like the Black Arts bumping auras with littlest Summers," Willow said gently.

She saw that Dawn totally picked up on the weird vibe. The girl muttered, "Yeah, whatever," and trudged away.

As Dawn entered the Magic Box, Tara murmured, "How can she not be real?"

Willow swallowed. *My question, too.* All she could think to say in reply was, "She's real. She's just kinda . . . new."

She finished the last symbol, completely the circle around the shop. The circle flashed and disappeared.

For the time being, their work here was done.

But the weirdness is not done, Willow thought. *The weirdness is just barely beginning.*

What's wrong with me? Dawn wondered. *Do I have, like, spinach in my teeth? Which I would never eat anyway, but . . .*

She walked into the Magick Box, her home away from home, and saw Xander at the table. He was doing research, which he hated, with a million books piled all around him. *He looks really cute today,* she thought. Of course, to Dawn, Xander looked cute every day. *24/7/365,* she thought, sighing a little wistfully. Someday she'd get old enough for him and he'd realize she was the one.

His dumb girlfriend, Anya, was arranging mystical knickknacks. Dawn had already decided she would never own a store, even one as cool at the Magic Box, because it was too much like cleaning your room. Anya didn't seem to notice that, or else she didn't mind, which made her even weirder in Dawn's book.

"Hey," Dawn said, gesturing to Xander's books. "We on the case?"

Xander smiled like he was insane. "Yeah. Right on

top," he announced, the smile growing even wider. "Perched, ready for action. How's my sweet, fancy Dawn doing?"

He poked playfully at her, again, and again, and she began laughing because she was happy that he was acting normal and obviously very, very happy to see her.

"Fine," she giggled. "What's up with you? You get into the sugar again?"

Anya walked up, beaming like Xander had just asked her to marry him, which would be to barf. Dawn looked over at her as Anya kind of just stood there, staring at her. Anya was smiling so hard, it was a wonder that her teeth didn't shatter. Her eyes were practically spinning. At last she said, "You make a very pretty little girl!"

As she kept smiling, Xander came over to her and said, "Anya, you want to help me with that thing?"

Anya looked totally crazy with the joy as she said to Dawn, "Xander needs help with his thing!"

Off they hustled, and Dawn frowned after them. *Okay, that was strange. Maybe I have an incurable disease. Maybe I have a tumor, just like Mom, only in my case, they can't operate. Xander and Anya are acting just as weird around me as Tara and Willow. Am I horribly disfigured and they don't want to tell me? Do I smell?*

Giles and Buffy came in from the training room. As usual, Giles was carrying his journal. It seemed all he did was write in it. He put it on the counter as he said to Buffy, "I'm not sure our basic workout is challenging you anymore. Perhaps we should make it harder."

Buffy made grumpy face at him. "You always think harder is better. Maybe next time I patrol, I should carry bricks and use a stake made out of butter."

Maybe he's written down what's wrong with me in his journal, she thought. Or at least he's got a clue about it . . . unlike me.

They're all older than me, she groused, watching the bustle. *They always know stuff, do stuff, that they won't tell me about. I know Buffy's the Slayer and all, but still, I could help a lot more than they let me. I could, like, spy on that Glory chick or help Willow and Tara more or something. Buffy was practically my age when she started Slaying.*

Giles should understand most of all. He knows what it's like to be a kid like me. He's known Buffy for, like, ever.

She gave the notebook a look. *It's gotta all be in there, what she was like, what kind of bad stuff she did. She always acts like she was never a kid. She's always so serious. And bossy. It would be so cool to dis her a little, let her know I know she wasn't always Miss Perfect . . .*

She put her backpack on the counter next to his journal and pulled out her notepad diary. Giles very casually closed the journal and picked it up.

Dawn was fascinated. *Did he do that because he didn't want me to see it?* she wondered. *Is he hiding something from me?*

"Very amusing," Giles said to Buffy. He smiled at Dawn, which worried her even more. "I bet Dawn feels like that with her school work sometimes."

Buffy said, "Hey, Dawn, that true? How was school today?" Her sister sounded far more normal than anyone else so far.

"The usual," Dawn replied. "A big square building filled with boredom and despair."

"Just how I remember it," Buffy tossed off.

Meanwhile, Giles moved behind the sales counter with his journal. Dawn tried to get a better look at it, but just then Buffy chose to ask her a question.

"So what's the homework sitch?"

"We're supposed to imagine what we'll be like in ten

years and write a letter to our future self. The teacher's so clearly out of ideas." She rolled her eyes, then added a little hopefully, "Wanna help?"

"Maybe later," Buffy said, but her voice got kind of wobbly. "I've got a few things to take care of."

Dawn glanced back to Giles, who was fiddling at a shelf on the wall behind the counter. His journal was nowhere to be seen.

Finally Dawn had had enough. "Is it about that weird girl who came to the house?" she asked sharply.

"Glory. And no, it's not," Buffy answered, looking all parental and put-upon. Dawn realized that her sister didn't get that she was asking about all the attitude around her, not what the few things were that Buffy was gonna take care of.

"Like you'd tell me, anyway." She rolled her eyes and moved into snotty sister mode. "'Dawn's too young. Dawn's too delicate—'"

"Right. A young delicate pain in the butt," Buffy retorted, and that made things a little better. *'Cause if I did have an incurable disease, Buffy wouldn't be so mean to me.*

So she gave it back, as good as she got.

"I think you're just freaking out 'cause you have to fight someone prettier than you. That's the big crisis, isn't it?"

Buffy gave her The Look, the one that said, *Don't even try to be as snotty as I can get. I will always win.* "Dawn, Glory is powerful, evil, and is in no way prettier than me."

Dawn opened her diary. "Maybe you're just getting soft in your advanced age. She didn't look that tough to me."

She loved the soft little "humph" that that drew out of her sister. Just loved it.

* * *

Orlando would have loved to die. And as the evil Hellgod smeared his blood across his lips and told him how wonderful it was that the people on "this backwater plane of existence" bleed, he wished with all his soul that he could make his heart stop.

Her minions had skewered his hands above his head with his own sword, pinning him to a column. She had tortured him, or had him tortured—he could no longer remember—and he was in mind-numbing pain.

For the glory of God, he reminded himself, and dedicated his agony to that of the Living Lord.

His blood trickled down his battered face, and Glory leaned in close. He was terrified.

"Now, one more time. Just between me and you. Our itsy-bitsy little secret. Where . . . is . . . the Key?"

"Even if I knew . . ." He hoped he was smiling defiantly. He could no longer tell what his face was doing. . . . "I'd die a thousand deaths before I tell you."

She circled around him like a lion sizing up its prey. From her body emanated a coldness that froze the breath in his lungs. She was evil incarnate, the beast made flesh, everything he had ever sworn to fight. And she knew it.

"Won't need a thousand, sweetie," she whispered into his ear. "I'll make the first one last. Long time. Even if you don't know anything."

Orlando stared back at her.

She flared with frustration. "What is it with you religious types?" Then she smiled. "It's intimacy, isn't it. Aww, you're just scared of letting someone in."

She pressed up close, dripping sex. He had not been with a woman in his entire life. He would live and die untouched.

"Sssh, it's okay. I know how hard the first time can be." She began to tremble. Orlando was certain why, but he couldn't believe it was from sensual desire. Then she ran her hands up his body, in a mockery of the things men and women do to each other for pleasure.

"You don't have to be afraid. Just relax. You may not have the info I want, but you've still got something I need."

Then she touched her fingertips to his temples. He stared into her eyes and he saw—

Suns and moons, comet-hot and white-spinning; kaleidoscopic shards of other places other times, other tortured men and women and then it all slid away, all of it . . . he was gibbering, he heard himself gibbering . . . the pain was hideous, it was unbelievable, unimaginable, let me die let me die it's. . . .

It's . . . .

A voice echoed: "Mmmm. Righteous."

God, Orlando thought. It was his last word.

Glory was finished.

Okay, glad for the party after all, Buffy thought, as she said happily, "Presents!"

The coffee table of the Summerses' living room was stacked with brightly wrapped gifts, surrounded by Buffy's favorite people, all asmile for her big night. Dawn was curled up with Joyce, a bit removed from the rest. Overhead, a banner read HAPPY BIRTHDAY, and Buffy couldn't help but think about last year, when Ethan Rayne had decided to give her Demon Giles as a gift.

Well, he's stuck in the desert, Riley's gone, and fun will be had by the rest of us, Buffy vowed.

As if to echo her thoughts, Willow said, "See? Just what you needed."

Buffy grinned back at her still-best friend. *After five years,* she thought, *Willow's very different, and still very much the same. Wow, and me without a single philosophy class under my belt.* "You are very, very wise," Buffy informed her. "Now gimmie gimmie gimmie!"

Buffy tore into Box #1 with all the joy of someone much younger than herself—*say, me a day ago. Maybe it'll be shoes!*

"This is extremely suspenseful," Anya announced. Then she blurted, "I want the presents!"

Grinning, Buffy pulled out a lovely, feminine dress. "Pretty," she said admiringly. "Thank you!"

Tara and Willow were pleased. "We thought you'd get a lot of crossbows and other killy stuff."

"So we figured, less killy, more frilly."

"It's lovely," Anya cooed. "I wish it was mine!" Then, fielding the looks of the rest of the gang, she said disdainfully, "Oh, like you weren't all thinking the same thing."

"I'm fairly certain I wasn't," Giles drawled.

Then Dawn thrust a small, hastily wrapped gift at her big sisters. "Open mine," she ordered.

Buffy feigned dubious concern as she accepted the package and began to open it. "It's not going to explode, is it?"

Once unwrapped, the gift hit Buffy hard. It was a picture of her and Dawn laughing and hugging each other on the beach, in a frame adorned with seashells. Dawn had clearly decorated the frame herself.

Buffy couldn't speak. She couldn't cry.

"It's when we visited Dad that summer in San Diego. I put the shells on myself. They're the ones we picked off the beach."

"Yeah," Buffy managed to say. "I . . . remember." *And I do. That's the thing. I remember every day of every year that we've been together.*

Except we haven't.

The room fell deathly quiet as everyone else picked

up the vibe. Dawn shifted uncomfortably and said, "Jeez, don't get all Movie of the Week. I was just too cheap to buy you a real present."

Buffy was moved beyond her capacity to explain. Her eyes welling with tears, she hugged Dawn closed. "Thank you," she said feelingly.

So, gift a hit, Dawn thought to herself. *Almost weirdly so.* The party had broken up into clumps, like they were doing a group discussion session at school. Everyone had a chat buddy except her.

She wandered toward the kitchen. Mr. Giles, her mom, and Buffy were in there. Her mom was saying, "It still sounds to me like there's a lot you don't know about this. I mean, is she . . . is she . . . dangerous?"

Buffy said quickly, "No."

Mr. Giles spoke up. "Well, let's wait a second on that. I assume you're asking about her existence, not her intentions . . ."

Buffy moved a little and saw Dawn.

Drat.

"Dawn? What you doing?" she called, her voice a little too loud and a little too shrill. "Party getting slow out there?"

I am extremely good at this, Dawn reminded herself. She managed to sound perfectly casual as she said, "We need plates. It's cake time." To illustrate her point, she grabbed some plates off the table and headed smoothly into the foyer.

She meandered into the living room, admiring Buffy's cool haul of stuff: some weapons, some clothes, a few books. Willow and Tara were at the coffee table, cutting Buffy's birthday cake with a sharp, gleaming knife. Willow laughed, licking a bit of stray frosting from Tara's finger.

Dawn put down the cake plates and kept going, over to where Anya and Xander stood. They were laughing and whispering to each other—*And why am I not surprised that the minute I come close, they immediately stop and look guilty?*

Totally frustrated, she said, "Why does everybody start acting all weird when I'm around?"

"Me? Me not weird," Xander argued, looking and sounding incredibly weird—which, okay, *Xander,* but still—weirder than usual.

"I'm not an idiot," Dawn said. "I know you're talking about me."

Xander and Anya shared a look that looked pretty real and honest, then both looked back at her.

"No. No, we really weren't," Xander insisted.

"We were talking about sex," Anya offered helpfully, and Xander blushed, just like he would if they really had been talking about sex.

Just then, Buffy came in. Mr. Giles and their mom followed close behind.

"They were talking about me," Dawn told her mom. "Just like everybody is."

"Again, not so much," Xander countered. "In fact, none."

Anya said to Joyce, "We were talking about sex. You know us. Sometimes we pretend stuff."

Joyce looked embarrassed and said, "Um . . ." as Xander said, "Anya—"

But the ex-demon didn't hear them. "Like, say, there's a fireman? Or a shepherd?"

Buffy's cheeks turned pink. "Okay, you know what? Let's not have this exchange of images right now."

And Dawn got pissed. Because, okay, maybe they weren't talking about her—she couldn't be sure, but that didn't mean she wasn't *not* sure. If that made any sense.

And if it does, then there's, like nothing any of them can say around me because I'm too young to live, and I might as well stab myself in the ears with a pencil because I might as well be deaf.

"Oh. Right." Her voice was shrill. "Of course. Can't let Dawn hear *anything*. Fine. I'll just go to bed. That way I won't accidentally get exposed to, like, *words*."

Dawn stormed off up the stairs. She was aware of a silence behind her, and then Willow asking the others, "Cake?"

Talk about lame, Dawn thought, and slammed her door.

She stood in the center of the room, fuming. *I'm not a little kid,* she thought. *And I'm not a stupid moron. They're keeping something from me. All of them.*

I'm going to find out what it is.

Spike the Vampire stood in the shadows at the back of the house on Revello, havin' a cigarette, watching the general merriment of the Slayer's twentieth birthday party through the windows. He felt supremely sorry for himself.

When Charles Dickens wrote those novels about the orphans always looking in, never part of the fun, he was thinking about me. Okay, not me precisely, but he knew about the loneliness of the human heart. Or the unbeatin' vampire heart. At any rate, he got it, and God, she looks good enough to eat tonight. Not that I would bite her, even if I could. Unless she wanted me to . . .

Whomp! Spike watched in fascination as Summers the Younger emerged from the shrubberies, obviously having just shimmied down the trellis outside her window. He had clearly startled her, and she tried to recover with a snotty, "Jeez! Lurk much?"

"Wasn't *lurking*," he said, hearing the defensiveness

in his voice. "I was standing about. It's a whole different vibe."

"What is—" she began, then stopped dead—*well, not exactly* dead—when she saw the candy box under his arm. "Are you giving Buffy a *birthday present?* Oh, my god, weird! Plus, chocolates? Lame! And the box is all bent and you know she'd never touch anything from you, anyway."

Supreme self-pity morphed into supreme irritation. He advanced on the chit and growled, "Shouldn't you be tucked away in your beddy-bye, all warm and safe where nothing can eat you?"

And back to self-pity as she laughed and said, "Is that supposed to scare me?"

Oh, God, I'm such a wanker. "Little tremble wouldn't hurt."

"Sorry." Her big eyes sparkled. "It's just . . . come on. *I'm* badder than you."

"Are not." He thought back to that rare and special time when he had almost managed to dust himself, and wished he had done.

"Am too." She gestured at him. "You're standing in the bushes hugging a bent box of chocolates. I'm—" She hesitated.

"What? Sneaking off to braid hair and watch the Teletubbies with your mates?"

"No," she insisted. "I'm breaking into the magic shop. To steal things." She narrowed her eyes as if to prove she was a real mean little bugger.

He pondered that. "Magic shop, eh? All number of beasties between here and there. Bet they'd really go for a Little Red Riding Hood like you. I bet that wouldn't set too well with your big sister."

"I can take care of myself," she snipped. Then she eyed the deep, dark, scary night—Spike's home away from home. He could almost see her wheels turning, as if to say, *On second thought* . . .

"Wanna go steal some stuff?" she asked him.

"Yeah, all right," he told her, flicking his cig on the sidewalk.

They skulked very skulkily, Spike being the king of sneakin' about and all that, and he got them to the Magick Box intact, and even with the bonbons unsullied in their box. He had nearly chosen to forget that it was the same box he'd used to pummel the likeness of Buffy he'd done up—*did the pummeling in a small fit of temper*—and figured that giving them to Buffy would smooth that out, in some way. *Not sure how, but* . . .

Li'l Bit was nervous as he picked the lock, acting as lookout. "You know how to do that or not?"

"Give us a sec," Spike said. "I usually just burst through doors."

Then, click! It came open, and Spike gave her a grin as she smiled at him in admiration.

"That's right," he said proudly. "Who's bad now?"

They went in, and Buffy's sister pulled a flashlight from the pocket of her jacket and made a beeline to the counter. She went round it, to a shelf on the wall behind the counter. Spike was intrigued. He carried his chocolates over.

"Girl with a mission, eh? So what's the caper? Jewels? Mystical artifacts? Or just plain hard cash liberated from the till?"

She said, "A book."

"All this for a book?"

He was monumentally disappointed. There wasn't much excitement in stealing a book, at least to his way of thinking. He spied an ornate crystal, liked it, and stuck it in his pocket.

"I don't want the book, just what's inside. I think it was Giles's notes. He was standing here with it but when I turned around it was gone . . ."

She fiddled about. Spike concentrated on smoking and lurking, then there was a *fwap* or a *zing* or somethin' and Dawn was looking right proud of herself. She had notebooks in her arms.

Hunh. Maybe life is like a box of chocolates after all, Spike thought.

Dawn had lit some candles because she was afraid to turn on the lights. She was also concerned that Mr. Giles would be able to tell that she had opened up the secret compartment behind the counter. But it was too late to worry about any of that.

So she munched the chocolates that Spike had planned to give to Buffy—they weren't the best, but maybe he didn't have a sense of taste; she'd heard that about vampires—and Spike was smoking—*gross habit, no wonder he's dead*—and sat listening while Spike frowned at the most recent of Giles's incredibly boring journals and puffed away, adding to the air pollution of the planet.

"Where'd he learn to write so bloody small?" Spike grumbled. "From a fruit fly?"

Dawn was looking over his shoulder, and she pointed at the page he was on and said, "Wait. Here's something. 'Tarnis, twelfth century. One of the founders of the Monks of the Order of Dagon. Their sole purpose appears to have been as protectors of the Key.'"

Spike sneered. "Brown robe types are always protecting something. Only way they can justify giving up girls."

He wandered over to a shelf and brightened. "Hey. Troll hammer," he announced.

It was a very large hammer, which confused Dawn, because she couldn't figure out why some trolls were big and some were small, and then she realized she was thinking of gnomes. *Being the Slayer's sister makes life very strange, and I wish I could get credit at school for knowing some of this stuff. It's not like I'm going to save the world by knowing all the state capitals.*

He moved to pick it up, straining under the weight, barely managing to set it back down without dropping it. "Doesn't go with my stuff, anyway," he groused.

Dawn went back to reading. "'The Key is not directly described in any known literature, but all research indicates an energy matrix vibrating at a dimensional frequency beyond normal human perception. Only those outside reality can see the Key's true nature.' Outside reality?" She glanced at her partner in vandalism. "What's that mean?"

Spike tossed his cigarette butt into an ornate urn. "Second sight blokes, maybe. Or even just your run-o-the-mill lunatics."

Crazy people?

Dawn tensed as memories flashed through her mind:

On the corner around from the Magick Box, a crazy man had wandered up to her. He stared at her hard, his eyes widening, and then he started shouting, "You don't belong here!"

Then there was the night watchman, who had been brought into the hospital, while Dawn and Buffy waited for their then-sick mother. He had stared at her, yelling, "There's no one in there!"

Everyone tried to tell me that those guys were saying those things because they were crazy. But both of them said those things to me. About me.

Spike was unaware of her freak-out. She wasn't sure she wanted to read anymore, but he said, "What else does it say about this Key? Is it made of gold? Might be able to hock it, split the take."

Dawn silently tried to clear her throat, which had become very dry and very constricted. A dark, oily feeling uncoiled in the pit of her stomach as she stared down at the letters of Mr. Giles's miniature handwriting.

"'The Key is also susceptible to necromanced animal detection, particularly those of canine or serpent construct . . . '"

Not long ago, an enormous snake monster had attacked her in this very store. It had been huge, and followed her and only her, like it was hunting her . . . like she was its prey.

The dark, oily feeling got worse, and she was afraid she was going to throw up.

Impatient, Spike leaned over her shoulder. "'The Monks possessed the ability to transform energy, bend reality . . . blah blah blah.' Good Lord, Giles writes as dull as he talks, doesn't he?"

He went on.

"'They started work, but the Council has suggested to us that they were interrupted, presumably by Glory. They obviously did manage to accomplish the . . . taste'?" He squinted. "'Accomplish the *task*. They had to be certain the Slayer would protect it with her life. So they sent the Key to her in human form . . . in the form of a sister.'"

The world broke.

Everything broke.

Her heart . . .

It's true. Somehow I knew it. Oh, God, oh, my God. I'm not . . . I'm not here . . .

"Huh," Spike said. "I guess that's you, nibblet."

Buffy's birthday party was drawing to a close, and the energy level in the Summerses' living room was going down like a slow-leaking balloon. Buffy was grateful for the sympathetic sad faces offered by her mom, Willow, and Tara, but she would have preferred a birthday remembrance from Riley. However . . .

Tactfully, Willow murmured, "Not even a card, huh?"

Buffy had a sad face also, but she tried to lighten it up. "I wasn't really expecting one. No contact with civilians. I'm sure there's a code name for it." She made air quotes with her tone of voice. "Like 'radio silence.' It's 'greeting card silence.'"

"Sorry," Willow said.

Buffy wanted to be a brave soldier. She sighed ruefully and said, "Maybe it's time for a new tradition. Birthdays without boyfriends. It can be just as fun."

Willow smiled at Tara, who grinned back. "Preaching to the choir here, baby."

"Yeah," Tara chimed in, "some of my best . . . *oh, god* . . . "

Buffy followed the line of sight of the horrified witch.

The room went stone silent, in utter disbelief.

Her baby sister, Dawn, stood on the other side of the room. Her right arm was extended, and blood was dripping from a gash across her palm. She had used the birthday cake knife to slash herself, and it hung limply in her other hand, like a dead thing. But the look on her face was worse; the horror there, and the agony . . .

Her voice . . . there was no sound in the world as roaring with pain as Dawn's voice, as she choked out, "Is this blood?"

"Dawn!" Buffy's mom cried.

Buffy rushed over and grabbed the knife away. *"What did you do?"*

"It's blood, isn't it?" Dawn ground out. "It can't be me. I'm not a Key. I'm not a *thing* . . ."

The horror turned to shock, all around.

She knows. Buffy trembled as if someone had thrown her into a frozen river. She had never been so cold in her life, so numb, so unable to move. *Oh, God, Dawn knows . . .*

"Sweetie, no," Joyce Summers began. "What is this all about?"

But her face put the lie to her words. Dawn broke down, sobbing.

"What am I?" she demanded, heartbroken. "Am I real? Am I *anything?*"

Joyce rushed to her, hugging her close, grabbing her small, fragile hand to stop the bleeding. She shared a devastated look with her older daughter, who was reeling. Beneath the numbness, anger seethed, propelled by her helplessness to spare Dawn this agony. Balling her fists, she wanted to break something as she thought, *It wasn't supposed to happen this way.*

A few minutes later, everyone left. Willow gave Buffy a tight hug and said, "Whatever you need, just—"

"Thanks," Buffy managed, as the two witches left together.

Oh, my poor, dear girl. And at her birthday party, too, Giles thought sorrowfully as he lingered, observing Buffy, admiring her ability to remain composed. *If one can call this somber affair a party any longer. It's more like a wake . . . for a little girl upstairs who must be very terrified.*

His slayer was frightened, too, and Giles moved to deal with that, deeply affected by her pain.

"Perhaps I should stay," he ventured at the front door. "Just in case . . ."

Buffy gave her head a shake. "This is family stuff," she told him. "We need to deal with it."

With that, he was dismissed along with the others. He

gave her a nod to show that he understood, but he couldn't help wishing she had asked him to remain behind. The younger Buffy of old—even of last year—would have gone into his arms like a daughter and looked to him for help. And he would have gladly given it.

The starling is flown from the nest, he reminded himself, as he stood on the other side of the door. *My girl has gone and grown up on me, and that's as it should be. I won't always be here for her. I can't be. She has to handle what life throws at her.*

But, my God, can't the universe stop lobbing hand grenades, at least for one night of presents and sweets?

Mourning the loss of innocence—*for us all*—he walked down the porch and to his new car, which was not half as wonderful as his old car.

Times change.

He glanced up at the row of windows fronting the second story of the Summers home. False memories flooded his mind, so real that he could not deny their power, even though intellectually he knew they were lies: Dawn as a little girl, begging him to let her have another bowl of chocolate ice cream while he was sitting her one afternoon; Dawn's piano recital, when she made herself burp to get a laugh out of the audience; Dawn's first crush, on a boy named Ted, causing no end of eye-rolling between Buffy and Joyce, a reference to the psychotic robot Ted, who had dated Joyce.

All we are or seem, is but a dream within a dream, he misquoted Shakespeare, too upset to recall the precise words.

With the others gone, it was time to deal with her family. Buffy wished she hadn't asked Giles to leave. He was family, too.

But she sensed somehow that in this matter, she had

to take the lead. She was the one in charge, even if her mother was the parent.

But it's almost like I'm Dawn's parent, she thought. *I'm the reason she exists.*

And now she knows that. How can she stand it?

Buffy's gaze moved up the stairs, her face filling with dread. Her mom was in her sister's . . . in Dawn's room, and Buffy had no idea how they were dealing. Dawn had always been the mama's girl, so much younger when their parents split up.

None of it happened, Buffy reminded herself.

But it *had.*

She climbed the stairs and entered Dawn's room. The scene hit her hard: Dawn was lying on the bed, staring off into space. Her hand was bandaged, but that was the least of the damage. Joyce, registering Buffy's entrance, was gently stroking Dawn's hair.

"Why didn't you tell me?" Dawn asked in the same tight, agonized voice as before.

Buffy's mom traded a look with Buffy.

"We were going to," Buffy began. "We just—"

"We thought it would be better to wait until you were older," Joyce cut in, saving Buffy as she trailed off into the land of no excuses.

"How old am I now?" Dawn croaked.

"Fourteen." Joyce's voice was gentle but firm. "You know that."

Dawn shut her eyes tight. "No. The Monks. When did they . . ."

The question hung in the air, and Buffy hated that it was being asked, and that it had to be answered. She wanted with all her heart to not know that Dawn was the Key. She wanted to be duped by the universe. She wanted lies, and to tell her that the world was black and white, and that good always triumphed . . . .

"Six months ago," Buffy murmured gently.

Dawn was crushed. "I've only been alive for six months?"

"No, honey." Buffy's mom came to her rescue again, as the clear voice of compassion and reason. "You've been alive a lot longer than that to us."

"You don't know that. You don't know anything!" In her despair, Dawn wanted to wound someone, anyone. "I'm a Key. Everything about me's just . . . made up."

Buffy came to her, her heart aching, and tried to be as direct and caring as her mother had been. "Dawn, Mom and I know what we feel. I know I care about you, know I worry . . ."

"You worry 'cause you have to. I'm your job." The tears spilled down Dawn's face. "'Protect the Key,' right?" Her expression was one of pleading, of so very much needing to be loved for herself.

"No," Buffy shot back, keeping steady, knowing Dawn needed her to be honest . . . and to honestly love her. "I worry because my sister is cutting herself—"

"Yeah?" Dawn interrupted, as if she couldn't bear to listen. "How do you know? Maybe it's just another fake memory from my fake family." Dawn wept.

"Honey . . ." Joyce reached out to touch her. Dawn withdrew, out of reach. Buffy and Joyce both stared at her, and Dawn looked downward.

"Get out," the girl murmured.

Buffy extended her hand. "Dawn—"

"Get out!" Dawn shrieked. She completely, totally lost it. "GET OUT! GET OUT!"

The Scoobies sat pensively in the gloom of the Magick Box, Giles's heirloom clock providing counterpoint to the general heaviness of the group. No one spoke. No one knew what to say.

"Maybe we could . . ." Xander began, then shook his head, dismissing whatever thoughts he had.

The bell above the door jingled. Buffy entered, quiet, wan, and small.

Willow asked, "Buffy, is everything okay?"

Buffy avoided the question, and Giles longed to have answers for her inevitable question. Sure enough, she turned to him and said, "Did you find anything new?"

Giles flooded with sorry. "We're looking, but—"

"We need answers, Giles," she cut in, sounding both desperate and very much in command. "We need to find out everything about the Key. What's it for? Who created it?"

Xander added, "And why Glory's got a big girl god jones for it."

Buffy shook her head emphatically. "No. This isn't about her. It's Dawn. She deserves to know where she came from. She needs to know. Or . . . or it's just gonna eat away at her."

Giles eyed the *Book of Tarnis* and his journals, still strewn on the counter. His secret cubbyhole was still ajar, as he had found it when he'd discovered that the front door had been forced open.

"How did she find these?" he asked. "How did she even get in here in the first—"

Just then, Anya cried, "Eww!" She put her hand into an ornate urn and held up a cigarette butt. "Who's been using the Urn of Ishtar as an ashtray?" she demanded.

Giles looked at Buffy, whose face darkened. She set her jaw.

He very nearly pitied Spike, the only smoker among them, but he could not find it in his heart to do so.

I've never held much with the notion that black's not a color, Spike thought as he painted his nails a divine shade of ebony. *It goes with everything, especially . . . lots of other black, which is what I wear. Angel does, as well, and look at him, all the birds sighing after him like's Rudolph bloody Valentino, or—who's that wanker— Fabio.*

The crypt door crashed open, and Buffy stormed in. He was startled—and happy—but he kept his cool, drawling, "Mornin', sunshine. If you've come round for eggs and sausage, I'm fresh out . . ."

Buffy grabbed the lid of the tomb and, with one hard pull, yanked it out from under him. He fell in with a thud.

"Hey, careful!" He stood, facing her, and showed her his nails. "These are wet!"

Wham!

Buffy slammed the tomb lid straight into Spike's chest, pinning him in place. He was stuck, so Buffy could yell at him without a bit of distraction.

"You let Dawn find out like that?" Her voice shook, always a bad sign. "From books and papers? You hate me that much?"

He struggled manfully not to show how much that particular blow hurt. 'Cause it did.

'Cause he fancied her. . . .

"I was just along for the ride," he informed her. "Not like I knew she was the mystical glowy Key thing. Nobody keeps me in the bloody loop, do they?"

Buffy looked like she was about to stake him, which she could do, and he wasn't so sure he'd stop her at the moment.

"You could have stopped her. You could have—"

And that, coupled with his own remorse, snapped him. He got angry back.

"Oh yeah, here it comes. Something goes wrong in your life, blame Spike. News flash, Blondie . . ."

In a single burst of strength and anger, Spike flipped

the tomb lid off and away from him. It landed with a heavy crash beside them, raising a cloud of non-vampiric dust that neither of them noticed much.

" . . . if kid sis wants to grab a midnight stroll, she'll find a way, sooner or later. I just thought she'd be safe with the Big Bad looking over her shoulder.

Hit home, I did, he thought, as he watched Buffy back off a bit. But she was still angry. *So now we share a moment of tension, until she says—*

"She shouldn't have found out like that."

But now she had him going, and he wasn't about to get in her kicks and licks without him paying her back a little. So he pointed at her and said, "You didn't think you could hide the truth from her forever, did you? Maybe if *you* had been honest with her in the first place, you wouldn't be trying to make yourself feel better with a round of Kick the Spike."

Buffy locked eyes with him, and if looks could kill . . . *good thing I'm already dead.*

"You have no idea how I feel," she said, turned, and left.

Spike deflated.

You don't either, Blondie, he thought morosely. *No bleedin', soddin' notion whatsoever.*

My life has been so strange, Joyce Summers thought as she brushed her knuckles against her younger daughter's door. *Other women my age have much more ordinary problems . . . say, inoperable brain tumors . . . but I have to have two daughters, one of whom is a Vampire Slayer and the other, a figment of my imagination.*

Oh, Dawn, oh, my little baby. I don't care what they say; my body can still feel the pangs of bringing you into the world. You're my own, as surely as if you . . . you really . . .

She pushed open the door, wondering if her sleepless night showed on her face, wondering if Dawn would notice, or care.

"Honey? You're going to be late for school."

Dawn was awake but still in bed in her clothes from the night before; she'd dressed so carefully to impress Buffy and her girlfriends, wanting so much to be like her big sister. She didn't turn to face her mother.

"I'm not going. Blobs of energy don't need an education, do they?"

Joyce didn't know how to respond to that. She sat on the bed, gently stroking Dawn's hair. *Such beautiful hair. So shiny. Like Buffy's . . .*

"You want me to make you some soup? I think there's some chicken and stars."

Dawn jerked away and glared at Joyce. Her tears had long since drained, leaving behind a vast, deep emptiness that was strangely devoid of her rage. "I'm not sick!" she shouted. "I'm not anything!"

"Honey, calm down," Joyce implored. "I—"

"Don't tell me what to do," Dawn said. Then, her voice strangled with fury, she added, "You're not my mother."

Joyce visibly flinched. It was the hardest thing she had ever had to hear. Worse even than Hank saying, "I don't love you anymore." *Or when Buffy left, and I didn't know if she was alive or dead . . . because I still had hope. . . .*

Dawn rose and grabbed her backpack.

"I changed my mind. I'd rather be at school."

She left Joyce behind, devastated and numb.

All I'm good at is loving them, she thought, spinning with grief. *That's all I have to offer . . . to both of my daughters.*

People knew Ben as the nice orderly who had befriended the Summers girls when their mother had been admitted into the hospital for her brain disorder. What they didn't know was that he was much, much more.

They didn't know he was trying to protect the Slayer and her family . . . from himself, in a way. Ben had been created to imprison Glory, the Hellgod who had entered this dimension in order to find the Key. So far she had not succeeded, and while he was curious about the whereabouts of the Key, the longer she was thwarted, the better. Eventually, her window of opportunity would end. He looked forward to that time even though there was a chance her demise would mean his own, as well. Intellectually he knew he wasn't "real," but there was no way he could accept that. He had memories, feelings, a job he loved, and friends he liked. As far as he was concerned, no one got any realer than that.

Now he swept into the hospital mental ward with a tray full of pills and a smile. He announced to the agitated patients, "All right, fellas! Today we got greens and blues and hey! Chartreuse! It's a party."

The newest patient murmured, "It won't stick."

Ben turned. The man was strapped down, his ruined hands stitched and bandaged.

"The birds have been pecking too long," the man continued, and Ben's eyes went wide as he recognized the symbols tattooed on the man's face.

"Byzantium," he breathed.

"Yes," said a voice behind him. "They have arrived."

Ben whirled around, to find Glory's chief henchminion, Jinx, smiling at him. He looked as if he had been in a barroom brawl. Since that was unlikely, Ben concluded that he had gone up against some of the enemy . . . and prevailed.

"How many?" Ben asked. *Enough to kill you all?*

The minion eyed the Knight of Byzantium, who was strapped to his bed. "Their numbers are few, for the moment. But they'll grow. The Knights of Byzantium are like ants. First you see one. Then two. Then . . . the picnic's ruined."

He turned to Ben and said, very carefully, "No matter how many we kill, they'll keep coming, wave after wave. It's time to put old animosities aside. Your fate is directly tied to her magnificently scented Glorificus. She's been extremely forgiving of your considerable foibles up until now, but if you persist in your defiance, she'll be forced to—"

And Ben finally exploded, his pent-up fear and frustration boiling over. He had had it; he was sick and tired of being reminded what he was and what he wasn't, and he let Jinx have it.

"What?!" he shouted. "What is she going to do? Send a six-pack of minions to bore me to death? Glory can't lay a finger on me. You know it, I know it, *she* knows it. So save the threats—or I'll finish the job I started on your head."

Ben stormed out, brushing Jinx out of his way. The patients would have to wait for their meds. He had finally, totally, had it.

These things are real, Dawn insisted, pouring over her diaries, which were spread all over her bed. Remembering things. Reliving things. *Even with CGI and greenscreen, there are some things that happen and some things that don't.*

And I . . . happen.

There were pages and pages of diary entries chronicling her life. *If I didn't write them, who did? How can this not be real?*

She took a deep breath. Then she heard the muffled

sounds of Buffy and Joyce arguing downstairs, and tried to listen.

It was frayed-nerve city downstairs from Dawn's bedroom, as Joyce said frantically, "We can't just let her sit up there all alone."

Buffy replied, equally frantically, "She needs time, Mom. We can't force her to be all right with this."

"So that's your answer? Leave her alone and hope everything works itself out?"

"No," said Buffy, "but if I were her I'd want a little space right now to try to figure things out, not my mom and sister coming at me from all sides."

Joyce lowered her voice. Dawn couldn't hear what she was saying, so she slipped out of her room and crept into the hall. "Her school called today. She's been suspended. She told one of her teachers to . . ." There was a beat, and then she continued. "She's never used language like that before."

"She probably feels like she can say or do anything now. It won't matter because she's not real. We're not her family. We don't even know what she is."

Oh, my God. Buffy's words hit Dawn like a punch in the gut. *That's what she really thinks of me.*

I'm not real.

She retreated to her room, closing the door. Then she did a sweep across her room, taking in all the lies that were her life. Fury and despair welled up in her, the pressure building, until she exploded. *I am not real.*

She ripped down posters, tore up photos, destroyed everything that was perpetuating the illusion of her life. She tore her diaries to pieces.

I am not real.

The tears and the heartbreak and the terror were real; they were the truest things about her.

Everything went into the trash can: pages, papers, hopes, dreams.

I'm not real.

In the living room of the Summers home, the argument was escalating. Joyce, with all the pain and protective instinct of a mother, cried, "How can you talk about Dawn like she's a thing?"

"I'm not," Buffy defended. "I'm saying that's how she feels."

Joyce was frantic, but trying to keep herself composed. "Then we need to show her it's not true. She needs to know that she's still a part of this family and we love her."

"It's not that simple," Buffy insisted. "We're not going to fix this with a hug and a kiss and a bowl of soup. Dawn needs to know what she is. She needs real answers."

Joyce would not be mollified. "What she needs is her sister, Buffy. Not the Slayer."

And Buffy knew, with all the certainty of her calling, that in this case, her mother was tragically, desperately wrong. Dawn was not Buffy's sister. That was what Joyce wished, more than anything: that this "family business,: as Buffy had told Giles it was, revolved around simple mortal humans.

"Mom, the Slayer is the only thing standing between Dawn and a god from the Bitch Dimension that wants to stuff her in some kind of lock and give her a good twirl. I need to be out there doing my job or else—"

A piercing screech split the air. Buffy stiffened, her eyes going wide.

"Willow's spell. Glory . . ."

She headed for the stairs; her mother stopped her.

"Wait." Her panic grew. "It's not Glory."

Fire, Buffy realized. *The house is on fire.*

Buffy barreled up the stairs and smashed open the locked door to Dawn's bedroom. Splinters flew. Joyce was right behind her, and they both flew into the room.

Flames rose from Dawn's trash can, where she had set her diaries and posters on fire. The smoke detector was still screaming, but Buffy's anguished shout of "Damn it!" rose above it.

She poured water from a cup into it, smothered the flames, and quelled the fire as Joyce turned off the smoke detector. Buffy's face flashed with redhot anger.

"Dawn!" she bellowed, looking around for the culprit.

"Buffy," Joyce said, more quietly.

"No, Mom," Buffy insisted, shaking her head. "She could've burned the house down. *Dawn!*"

"Buffy . . ."

Buffy finally turned and took note of the stricken expression on her mother's face. Joyce Summers was reeling as she said, "She's gone."

The Slayer's gaze turned to Dawn's open window, and her face dropped.

From bad to apocalyptic in a heartbeat.

The Key staggered down streets it had been tricked into thinking it knew, past houses and street signs that had no bearing on its original plane of existence.

Nothing is certain, it thought in a language that was not its own.

And the Key, clothed in falsehood, disappeared into the deep, dark night.

The Scoobies assembled at the Magick Box as soon as Buffy called them, including a reluctant Spike. She could barely keep it together, but she managed it, and

Giles vowed then and there to back her up as best he could. One of the ways he could best serve the cause was to remain as logical as he could, seeking the truth of the situation.

"Willow's warning spell wasn't tripped? You're sure?"

"It wasn't Glory," Buffy replied firmly. "Dawn's been acting . . . It hasn't been easy for her. She tore her room up, burned all her diaries . . ."

The others were shocked. Xander blurted, "The Dawnmeister Chronicles?"

"But she's been keeping those since she was . . . I mean . . ." Willow was stricken.

Buffy gave her friend a nod. "Since she was seven. I remember, too, Will."

Then his slayer moved into combat mode, and Giles was proud of her. "We have to find her, fast. Before Glory or the Knights of Hack and Slash figure out what she—*who* she really is. Mom's at the house in case Dawn comes back there. The rest of us'll split up and sweep the city." She gave her attention to the pale, white-haired vampire and said, "Spike, reach out to your dank and darks, find out if they've seen—"

Spike looked supremely uneasy. "I'd love to help, but—"

"I'll pay you," Buffy informed him. "Just do it."

He gave his head a shake. "Chip in the head, sweetcheeks. Means I can't kill anything but demons. They didn't exactly vote me most popular this year." As the others frowned at him, he added, "Well, a fellah's gotta kill *something* . . ."

"Anya, stay put in case she shows up here," Buffy said. "Giles, Xander, sweep the center of town. Willow, Dawn, west side. Spike, you're with me on the east. We have to . . ."

She faltered. Giles wished more than anything that he could comfort her, but he knew she had to maintain her battle readiness.

They dispersed.

The Key drifted to the edge of Sunnydale Park. Staring at the swing set, it became lost in reverie, a memory seizing it like a living thing: a little girl, taunting her older sister—who was little herself—to push her higher on the swing.

It registered every detail, every taste, smell, sight, sound. Watched the movie the Monks had inserted into its consciousness, bewildered and heartsick.

Except that it did not have a heart, ordinarily.

Giles and Xander kept to the back alleys, Xander toting a long construction crowbar, and Giles armed with a sleek black crossbow.

The young man was having a difficult time accepting Dawn's reality. He said to Giles, "There are so many things I remember. Seeing Dawn, hanging with her, listening to Buffy complain about her. Mostly that last one," he added feelingly. "How could all of those things just . . . never have happened?"

"Takes getting used to," Giles agreed. "To think, that a bright fourteen-year-old is actually living energy, thousands of years old."

Xander took that in. "And I'm guessing some kind of superpowerful object in her raw form."

Giles nodded. "People have killed, died, and summoned armies to control the Key."

They kept looking, kept searching, as Xander said, "You know, she's, uh, kinda got a crush on me."

Giles glanced at him. "Your point being?"

Xander had the grace to look moderately embarrassed,

then obliterated any chance at humility he had, by saying, "Well, no, nothing, I'm just saying, powerful being, big important energy gal, diggin' the Xan-man. Some guys are just cooler, you know . . ."

Just when I think he's evolved, Giles thought, *he finds a way to reassure me that such a thing will never happen in my lifetime . . .*

. . . unless I turn out to be a Key as well . . .

Sighing, he led the way out of frame, still searching.

Willow and Tara combed the woods at the edge of town. There was a campfire, long since cold, but no sign of anything else. Whatever had been here was not here now.

"Maybe . . . maybe that way," Willow suggested, obviously running out of ideas.

Tara gently said, "We looked that way. And this way. And the other way. She's not out here."

Willow sagged, knowing Tara was right. "Where would you go?" she asked, profoundly worried. She stared into Tara's eyes. "If you felt lost and alone, where would you go?"

Tara took a moment, and then she did her best to wrap her dear, precious Willow in the hope that many, many things on this plane of existence were good.

She said, "To you."

"Dawn?" Buffy called into the darkness at the park. "Dawn?!"

"Yeah, that should do it," Spike drawled.

"Shut up."

"The nibblet scampered off to get away from you. She hears you bellowing, she'll pack it in the opposite direction. Can't say I blame her."

And it was about that, right now. Blame, guilt,

responsibility. Buffy had to protect the Key, but what she wanted to do was find her little sister.

She said to Spike, "You were right. It's my fault. I should have told her."

Humbled, dejected, she waited for Spike to let her really have it, give her a verbal punch when she was down and out. But he surprised her, as he did on occasion, by being kind to her in her moment of need.

"She probably would have skipped off, anyway, even if she never found out. She's not just a blob of energy. She's also a fourteen-year-old hormone bomb. Which one's screwing her up more right now? Spin the bloody wheel."

He raised his chin slightly and stared into the night, which was his time. His place. He said, "You'll find her, just in the nick of time. That's what you hero types do."

His voice was soft, sincere and, strangely, tremendously reassuring. "You'll find her."

"And then what?" Buffy demanded.

He had no answer for that one.

An ambulance siren wailed plaintively in the distance, a harbinger of injury, pain . . . and chances for salvation.

Dawn drifted on, a ghost in her own body. Past the Bronze, which was still open. Music and laughter vibrated inside. An ambulance screamed past, startling her; it was a counterpoint to the giddiness of young adults out on the town, in the night, making their own memories out of their friends, their feelings, their reality. . . .

But I do have some of that, she thought, an idea forming. *I have my own reality* . . .

She headed out, in search of one of them, half-staggering, half-plodding, down the streets that were only six months old for her. Past bushes, lampposts, fences that she remembered scaling in order to snitch avocados and oranges off the trees in people's yards.

Then she got to the place where the nightmare people lived: Sunnydale Medical Center.

The hospital was on the graveyard shift, eerily quiet and nearly deserted. Dawn slipped in and crept down a hallway, then through a door just as a nurse rounded the corner, wheeling a tray of what smelled like bedpans down the hall.

The mental ward housed four men, and as she drew near, she could hear their whimpering and muttering. She swallowed down her fear and came closer, staring at each of them in turn.

"It's here, it's here, it's here," one groaned.

"Make it stop," begged another. "The skin's too tight."

"Can't hear it," the first one muttered. "What's the frequency?"

It was to this one that Dawn was drawn. He reminded her of Santa Claus—*also a lie*—and he whimpered, trying to move away from her.

"Empty," he babbled. "All spilled out—"

"Please. You see me, right?" She pressed her lips together so she could stop her teeth from chattering. "Look at me."

The second crazy man whispered, "Can't stop."

Dawn stayed focused on the other one. "You know what I am, don't you? You all know. *Tell me.*" .

The man shook his head side to side, side to side, his features screwed up tight in extreme effort. "Can't hear it can't hear it can't hear it—"

"What am I?" Dawn pleaded.

"The Key!" someone cried.

Dawn whirled around.

This patient was younger than the others. There were strange markings on his face, which was quivering as he stared at her. His breathing was erratic, but his body was still. His face kept twitching, as if it was almost too much for him to say words that made sense.

"I found it," he said, on the verge of tears. "Thank you. Thank you."

Dawn walked to him. "You know what the Key is?" she asked. "Where did I come from? Who made me? What am I? *Please . . .*"

The patient's eyes crashed open as he writhed on the bed, his body jerking in the restraints. He was trying to get at her. "Destroyer! Cracked earth and bones!" he shouted. "The sun bleeding into the sky!"

Dawn shook her head. "No—"

"The Key is the link!" he yelled. "The link must be severed!"

Then all the men erupted into fits. Panicking, Dawn fled, throwing open the door . . . and running into a friend. Her own, real friend.

Ben.

Dawn sat with Ben in the break room, at a table with chairs among rows of lockers. As Ben bustled, making hot chocolate, she hunched over the tabletop, feeling small and young and alone and not at all like something that must be severed.

"Two steaming cups of chocolate goodness," he announced, setting down two mugs. "Courtesy of whoever I swiped it from out of the cupboard."

Dawn sat numbly, trying to register the fragrance of the cocoa. She was numb, inside and out.

"Couldn't find any marshmallows," he added, with mock apology. "I'll try to steal some for next time."

She said absently, "Don't like 'em anyway."

He laughed in disbelief. "What? Is that even possible?"

"Too squishy," she told him. "When I was five, Buffy told me they were monkey brains. . . ." *No, she didn't. She never did.*

He leaned forward, his face warm and gentle.

Vaguely she wondered why Buffy hadn't hooked up with him. He was a lot like Xander. She also wondered why Buffy had never hooked up with Xander, either.

"Dawn, was your mom brought back in?" he asked. "Is that why you're here?"

"No." She couldn't keep the bitterness out of her voice. "My 'mom' is just fine."

He stayed nice. "Is there anybody I can call? Your sister?"

Can I tell him? Can I tell anyone?

"I don't have a sister."

"Oh." He thought he got it. She could tell by the expression on his face. "You two have a fight?"

She didn't answer.

"It's okay," he assured her. "I know how that goes. I've got a sister, too. They can be a real pain sometimes, huh? I'll tell you, there's been a lot of nights I wish *she* didn't exist, either."

Dawn said miserably, "It's not Buffy. It's me. I'm the one that doesn't exist."

He was all big-brother, but without a clue. "Look, I know it can feel that way sometimes, but when you're older—"

"No, you don't understand!" she cried. "It's not real!" She gestured to her own body with loathing and despair. "None of this! They made it!"

Ben reached out a hand to her. "Dawn—"

"I'm nothing. I'm just a thing the Monks made so Glory couldn't find me! I'm not real!"

Ben stumbled back from the table, fearing tearing across his face. His eyes were huge.

"You're the Key?"

She was stunned. "How do you know about the—"

"Go," he said, wigging. His voice rose to a high-pitched yell. "Before she finds you. Don't ask me how she knows, 'cause she always knows. *Just go!*"

He was scaring her, big-time. More than the men in the mental ward had scared her. More than cutting herself had scared her.

She came toward him, arms outstretched. "Wait," she begged. "Calm down. Just tell me."

"You don't understand." He was panting with fear. His eyes darted right, left. "You're a kid. You stay, and she'll find you; she finds you, she'll hurt you—"

"What's wrong with you?" she demanded, her voice breaking as she began to lose it, too.

He shook his head violently, like the men in the mental ward. He was panting. He was barely keeping it together. "No no no no! You're what she's been searching for. I'm telling you, *run!* You don't know. You—"

Then he stiffened like he was having a total spaz-out seizure, going way over the edge.

"Oh, no. Oh, god, no. She's coming." He looked around like he could see something she couldn't. "I can feel it. You've got to get out. SHE'S HERE—OH, NO—"

He grabbed her.

"She's HERE!"

As he held Dawn in his arms, long curly hair sprouted from his head. His features stretched and changed. His body shifted, shortened, taking an altogether different human shape and keeping it.

Eyes . . . nose . . . mouth . . . ears.

Ben was Glory.

And Glory's arms were firmly wrapped around the quaking terror who was Dawn Summers. Who had just told the Hellgod that she was the Key—the thing Glory had been torturing and killing people to find.

Now Glory had the Key, literally in her grasp.

Dawn couldn't move.

She'll destroy me now, she thought. *Will it hurt?*

The god cocked her head and said brightly, "Hey. Don't I know you?"

Dawn stared at Glory, wondering if she was trying to make a sick joke. Then Glory released her and began to peel out of Ben's scrubs.

"Ugh, cotton," she said with disdain. "Could any fabric be more annoyingly pedestrian?"

The god banged open a locker and pulled out a red silk dress, tossing it over her naked body and letting it shimmy down over her chest and hips.

"Now this is what I'm talking about. Makes your skin sing!" she sang.

Dawn was sitting at the table—*how'd I get back to my chair?*—petrified, trying to send an SOS to Buffy, only ESP didn't run in the . . . she didn't have any superpowers that she knew of.

"You're . . . you're . . ." she began, but couldn't manage to make her mouth work.

Glory grinned at her expectantly and raised her brows. "Getting bored fast?"

"You're Ben?" Dawn blurted out.

Glory laughed. "It's an eensy more complicated than that. Family always is, isn't it?"

Dawn's eyes flicked to the door, gauging the distance. *If I run as fast as I can . . .*

With her back to Dawn, the Hellgod said cheerfully, "You'd never make it. I'd rip your spine out before you got half a step. Those little legs wouldn't be much good without one of those . . ."

Dawn jumped. Glory was suddenly standing right next to her. Dawn hadn't even seen her move.

" . . . would they, Dawnie?" Glory asked, all sweetness and death.

She smiled, hunkering down to eye level.

"Now, what I'm trying to noodle is what in the world the Slayer's little sis doing here with gentle Ben?"

It took Dawn a moment to understand, and when she did, she fought as hard as she could not to betray anything on her face, or in her reactions.

She doesn't know . . . doesn't know I'm the Key!

"You do-don't remember?" Her voice shook.

"Remember what?" Glory asked, looking unconcerned. "You were talking to him, not me." She leaned in, close and dangerous. "He wasn't being naughty, was he?"

Then there was a big, chubby guard, and he walked in, and Dawn's mind raced ahead to him calling for backup, and stunning Glory with a special gun, and her winding up in handcuffs and cursing them all, swearing to get them for this, and they hauled her off to a special, secret detention center, and Buffy and Ben sent her back in the transporter to her own dimension, where she floated in a bubble for all eternity, shrieking and pounding the sides, trapped—

Only it didn't happen that way.

The guard said, "Excuse me, ma'am? This area's for hospital personnel only. I'm going to have to ask you to—"

Glory grabbed the guard's head and gave it a sharp twist. Dawn gasped in horror and shrank away. The guard went down, his head twisted at a very wrong, very unnatural angle.

"Rude!" Glory snapped. "I'm talking here." She fluffed her hair, composed herself, and gave Dawn a huge smile.

"What do you say we find someplace off the beaten so we can have a nice, long *uninterrupted* chat, girl to god?"

Dawn wanted very badly to go insane, to shake her head and say, "Can't hear it can't hear it can't hear it."

But that gift was not forthcoming. Life, yes. And perhaps death.

But not insanity.

* * *

Shady Hill was tonight's meeting place of the Scoobs—it being not an unusual thing for them to meet in one of Sunnydale's dozen cemeteries—as Willow and Tara joined up with Buffy and Spike.

No joy: "We looked," Willow reported sadly, "but . . . no Dawn."

Buffy was not about to give up without a fight. She said, "What about the carousel?"

"We checked there, too." Willow sighed, and Tara looked mournful and very, very worried.

Then Giles and Xander arrived, also with the glum, and Buffy had to ask, just in case she had suddenly lost the power to interpret all forms of nonverbal communication. "Nothing?"

"I'm sorry, Buff," Xander told her.

Buffy's heart sank, and she was forced to go where she so did not want to go.

"Anything could have happened to her. I mean, not just Glory . . ." She took a breath, exhaling slowly, but her chest would not push out the air. It was just too tight. "We'd better check the hospital."

Glory dragged Dawn into a deserted X-ray room. In her tight red silk dress, the Hellgod was admiring the X rays, or pretending to, or Dawn didn't know what. Half of her wanted someone to walk in and save her, while the other half understood that any human being who walked through the door would be dead within five seconds.

Except maybe not my . . . the Slayer.

"Now this one!" Glory said, bending for a better look at the X ray. "Oh, I really think they've captured something here. I just love seeing what's on the inside of people. Although I usually prefer a more hands-on approach."

She whipped around and looked at Dawn, whose stomach did a flip.

"Okay! Small talk over. I'm in a bit of a crunch here, so let's cut right to the ooey gooey center. Your sister, the Slayer, has my Key. It's mine. I want it. Do you know where she squirreled it away?" With a vicious but sweet smile on her face, she drawled, "There's ice cream and puppy dogs in it if you start singin'."

Dawn swallowed down her fear and stammered, "I- I'm not sure. What's it look like?"

Glory smiled and looked pensive. "Well, let's see . . . the last time I got a peep, it was a really bright green swirly shimmer. Really brought out the blue in my eyes. But then those sneaky little monks pulled an abracadabra, so now it could look like anything. You see my predicament?"

Dawn carefully gauged the situation . . . and saw a way to play it to her advantage. Lowering her gaze, she said thoughtfully, "Maybe . . ."

Glory leaned in expectantly. "Yes?"

"Maybe if you told me more about it, I'd know if I've seen it," she suggested.

Glory stared at her, her face unreadable. *Oh, God, can she read my mind?* Dawn wondered.

Then the god brightened and said, "Okay!"

Once at the hospital, Giles allowed himself to stay in the background as Buffy spoke to the admitting nurse. Then she rejoined the group, her face grave, and Giles, along with everyone else, tensed.

"She wasn't brought in," Buffy told them.

The tension level receded not in the slightest. "That's a happy thing, right?" Xander asked.

Buffy was nearing meltdown. "I don't know. I can't . . ."

Before Giles could move to comfort her, a hospital

worker of some sort rushed past with two security guards. He was shaking as he said, "I found him up on the third floor in the break room! Jesus, you gotta see him! His head's almost twisted clean off!"

Buffy looked frightened and very determined. She said one word: "Glory."

And then she was off.

With the others, Giles followed.

Dawn was getting somewhere with Glory, but now she knew what those little mice at the Sunnydale Pet Shoppe felt like when they got plunked into the cage with the snakes. She wanted to run, but then the serpent would strike. But it was all she could do to stay in the room, in case the serpent struck, anyway. Without warning . . .

"So this Key thing," Dawn drawled. "It's been around for a long time?"

Glory considered. "Not as long as me, but yeah. Just this side of forever."

Dawn tried to understand that. Then she asked the question she did not want to ask, but had to ask, must know:

"Is it . . . evil?"

"Totally," Glory chirped.

Dawn reeled.

"Well, no, not really. I guess it depends on your point of view."

Glory twitched just for a second, as if she was working a kink out of her neck. Dawn was trying not to pass out, because it was just too hard to breathe, but this might be the only chance she ever had to find out who . . . *what* . . . she was.

"What's it for? I mean, if it's a Key, there's gotta be a lock, right?"

Glory spiraled in a circle. "Yes! We have a winner!"

"So, what does it open?"

And maybe she asked the question too fast, or maybe Glory was paying better attention, but something went wrong. Because instead of answering, the Hellgod narrowed her eyes.

"I smell a fox in my henhouse!" she accused. "Is that why you were playing sugar and spice with Uncle Ben? Trying to get a peek at Glory's unmentionables?"

Trembling, Dawn shook her head, pulling into herself. "No, I—"

"Shhh! I kinda want to hear me talking now." She wagged a finger at Dawn. "Me talking." She gave Dawn a quick, sharp nod as she considered her carefully. "You know what I'm starting to think? I'm thinking that maybe *you . . .*"

Oh, God. She knows. She's figured out I'm the Key.

" . . . don't have any idea where my Key is," Glory flung at her. "Very irritating. Irrational. You know what I mean, tiny snapdragon?" She made claws out of her nails and started scratching her arms. "Like bugs under my skin, and, say, I'm feeling a little . . ."

She drifted off, swaying. Dawn was almost more frightened of her then, than when the god had advanced on her.

"What's wrong with you?" Dawn demanded.

"Hey!" Glory announced, with sudden insight. "This doesn't have to be a complete waste of my precious time! I've been meaning to send the Slayer a message, and I could use a little pick-me-up." She smiled happily. "Two birds, one stone, and boom!" She smashed her hands together, and Dawn jumped, bursting into tears. "You've got yummy dead birds."

She reached for Dawn's head. The Key was weeping now, whimpering, begging for her life, for her sister, for help of any kind—

And then the beloved voice came:

"Get away from my sister."

The Hellgod whirled around. Buffy faced her off, and Giles stood with the others, at the ready.

"Oh, hey!" Glory cried, delighted. "We were just talking about you!"

"Conversation's over, Hellbitch," Buffy said ruthlessly.

She attacked with a ferocity Giles had seldom seen. She employed a stick and move strategy, hitting Glory hard and dodging her counterattack. The rest of the gang fanned out across the room as Spike joined Buffy in pounding her.

Sneering, Spike said, "I though you said this skank was tough?"

Wham! Glory swatted the vampire across the room. Spike hit a wall, and then the floor, unconscious.

She said to Buffy, "If he wakes up, tell your boyfriend to watch his mouth."

Giles thought, *Oh, dear . . .*

Predictably, the implication that Buffy would actually find someone like Spike to be worthy of her romantic interest resulted in massive payback, as it were.

She bellowed, "He's! Not! My! BOYFRIEND!"

Buffy pummeled Glory with the fury of a hay thresher set on puree. The two clashed like Titans, and Giles awaited his cue.

Willow and Tara, who had positioned themselves on opposite sides of the room, closed their eyes as they quietly chanted. Giles felt magick charge the air.

Also, Buffy and Glory were in the air, slamming and ramming into each other as they battled. The Hellgod grabbed onto Buffy's foot in mid-kick, and gushed admiringly, and with apparent genuine admiration, "Hey, those are really nice shoes!"

Buffy back-flipped, catching Glory in the chin with

her free foot. Then Buffy crashed to the floor and shouted, "Giles! Now!"

Giles raised and aimed his crossbow. Then he fired. The bolt slammed into Glory's chest . . . and bounced off.

"Oh, please!" Glory snickered. "Like that's gonna—"

Xander attempted to clock her in the head with his crowbar. It bent . . . she didn't.

"Hey!" she shouted. "Watch the hair!"

She grabbed the crowbar hard, sending Xander sailing into Giles. Then she hefted the crowbar like a spear. Giles was rather put in mind of the Amazons, who had actually cut off their left—

"Okay! Time to start the dyin'!" Glory hurled the crowbar . . . at Dawn.

"Dawn!" Buffy shouted.

The Slayer leaped into the way at the last second. With the sickening sound of tearing muscle and shattering bone, the crowbar impaled Buffy in the shoulder. She went down in agony, and Dawn ran to her side.

"Buffy!" Dawn shrieked.

"Nice catch!" Glory chortled.

"Get back," Buffy warned her sister. With strength of purpose beyond imagining, she yanked the crowbar out of her shoulder as Glory began a fresh attack.

"Is that the best you little crap gnats could muster?" she demanded, advancing on the fallen Slayer. "'Cause I gotta tell you . . . so not impressed."

Giles glanced at the two witches. Before Glory could reach Buffy, Willow and Tara suddenly sprang into action, throwing colored dust at the Hellgod from either side. It hit her and clung, staining her skin and clothes.

Glory was livid. "Look what you did to my dress, you little—"

Then Willow cried in Latin—*the Vulgate, and perfectly cognated*— "Begone!"

She slammed her hands together, activating her spell.

The great god Glory, ruler of a demon dimension, disintegrated in an astonishing and spectacular *magickus ex machina.*

Willow collapsed to the floor, blood streaming from her nose.

"Willow!" Tara cried, rushing over to her.

Buffy stared at Willow. "What did you do to her?"

Weakly, as Tara fussed over her, Willow replied, "Teleportation spell. Still working out the kinks . . ."

Buffy said, "Where did you send her?"

"Don't know," Willow admitted. "That's one of the kinks . . ."

*Heavy, heavy, hangs over
Sunnydale. . . .*

Glory started to re-form half a mile above the ground. She looked down at the twinkling lights of the city and grimaced, knowing what was to come, as she said, "Oh, sh——"

Which didn't begin to describe her fall.

As Dawn flung herself into Buffy's arms, Buffy cried, "Dawn!" and the two were reunited.

Giles helped Willow up, saying to her, "That's an incredibly dangerous spell for an adept at your level."

"Yep," said the red-haired Wicca, "won't be trying that one again soon."

Buffy pulled back from Dawn, checking her over to make sure she wasn't hurt.

"Are you all right? Did she hurt you?" Buffy demanded.

Dawn stiffened. "Why do you care?"

"Because I love you. You're my sister."

Dawn shook her head, once more awash in her own misery. "No, I'm not."

"Yes, you are," Buffy said emphatically. "Look."

She took Dawn's hand. The self-inflicted cut across Dawn's palm had opened up during the fight.

"Blood. Summers blood," Buffy said to her. Then she took her own hand and smeared blood from her shoulder wound on it. She held up her hand and said, "Just like mine."

Then she pressed her palm into Dawn's, mixing their blood together, saying, "It doesn't matter how you got here or where you came from. You are my sister. There's no way you could annoy me as much if you weren't."

All of Dawn's anger and defenses came crashing down. In a rush of hungry tenderness, she hugged Buffy tight and said, "I was so scared."

"Me, too," Buffy murmured.

Then Dawn's eyes widened. She said, "Wait! Ben! He—"

Confusion seized her. Giles watched with great interest. She was clearly trying to piece something together, which was now eluding her mental capacities. He didn't know if it was a function of her being the Key, or of shock, or a combination of several factors. But it bore noting.

In a journal which I shall hide more properly, he thought. *Or learn to write in a secret code, as Watchers once had done.*

"He was here," she said slowly, replaying the events in her mind. "He was trying to help me, but then he . . ." She frowned. "I think he might have left before Glory came." She was very puzzled. "I . . . I can't remember."

"It's okay," Buffy assured her. "We'll thank him the next time we see him." She smiled lovingly, adoringly, at her sister. "We'd better get back. Mom's freaking out."

Dawn clouded over, an adolescent suddenly faced with something more terrifying than an insane demon Hellgod. "Is she mad?" she asked in a small voice. "About the fire?"

Buffy smiled. "I think you sort of have a get-out-ofjail-free card, on account of big love and trauma."

"Really? Okay. Good." Dawn looked vastly relieved. She and Buffy moved on. As they went:

"Think she'd raise my allowance?"

"Don't push it," big sister replied.

Epilogue

And so ...

Giles opened his eyes. He was standing with his journal to his chest in the center of the firestorm; surrounding him, the flames crackled and raged, fireballing overhead in roiling green windwhips. Great whirlpools of orange, red, and yellow tumbled over and around him; there were funnels of fire, explosive clouds of it.

Then the demon's voice rumbled and shuddered beneath Giles's feet, and inside his head. It said:

You've outgrown your usefulness to her. She doesn't need you, and so your life in return for hers means nothing to me.

"She doesn't need me," Giles whispered, knowing it deep in his white-hot bones. *And that's as it should be,* he thought, proud and moved. *That is the dream of every ... parent.*

In the cool, green fires, Rupert Giles's eyes welled. *I*

am her father, in nearly every sense of the word.

What a wonderful life I have led. It's a life worth giving up for her . . . which is what any loving father would do for his child.

He stood in the fires alone for a time, and then the demon spoke again.

Your sacrifice would be in vain, the demon repeated.

"Are you trying to welsh?" Giles accused Krathalal. "Go back on your word?"

Speaking like that, you take your life in your hands, the Ravager of Souls threatened.

"It's still mine to give," Giles shot back. He raised his chin. "Conclude the pact, please."

It will not be necessary.

Buffy's fate is unique and independent of your own.

Giles was surprised . . . and a trifle afraid. He gazed at the flames as they undulated and caressed him, extending his hands and spreading his fingers. He felt no different. He felt unchanged. He was no longer bleeding.

Buffy would live. And so would he. The pact was null.

Slowly, Giles lowered his arms and began to walk through the fire.

It was only then that he realized his journal had disappeared from his grasp. He turned back, to watch it blazing in the flames, each page turning to ash.

He prayed that it was a portent of new pages added to Buffy's life, fresh lines upon which nothing had yet been written.

Her own journal, he thought.

As the fires consumed the last of his book, he turned back around, and continued on his journey.

I shall never be forgiven all my faults, by man

nor god nor
any
good
thing.

But this I know: I am not here for grace,
nor pardon,
nor to give them.
My way is through shadow,
blackness on the path, and in my
heart,
in my eyes,
and in my soul.

My fate . . .
unknown.
My destiny . . .
my own.

ABOUT THE AUTHOR:

Nancy Holder has written many projects for both the *BTVS* and the *Angel* television shows. She is currently working on a quartet of novels about rival witch families in Seattle. She lives in San Diego with her daughter, Belle, and a confederacy of critters: Dogs Dot and Ty-ty; Sasha and David, the cat sisters; finches Bekah and Zoe; and two frogs, as yet unnamed. Life is grand.

Buffy
the vampire slayer™

. . . A GIRL BORN
WITHOUT THE FEAR GENE

FEARLESS™

A SERIES BY
FRANCINE PASCAL

SIMON
PULSE

FROM SIMON PULSE
PUBLISHED BY SIMON & SCHUSTER

ANGEL™

INVESTIGATIONS:

WE HELP THE HELPLESS

"Los Angeles. It's a city like no other. . . . People are drawn here. People, and other things. They come for all kinds of reasons. My reason? It started with a girl."
—Angel, "City Of"

For a hundred years, Angelus offered a brutal death to everyone he met. And he did it with a song in his heart. A gypsy curse put a stop to his rampage, but his doomed love of Buffy the Vampire Slayer drove him from Sunnydale on his own quest for redemption.

Now, go behind the scenes with your favorite broody vamp for all of the exclusive dirt. Exclusive interviews with cast and crew, an introduction by Co-Executive Producer Tim Minear, episode "dossiers," character files, notable quotes, color photo inserts, and more!

Everyone's got their demons.

THE CASEFILES, VOLUME ONE
by Nancy Holder, Jeff Mariotte, and Maryelizabeth Hart
Available in April 2002

From Simon Pulse
Published by Simon and Schuster